MURDER CREEK

A Hanging at Bloody Harlan

* * *

*Inspired by actual characters and
events in 1930 Appalachia*

J. Kyle Johnson

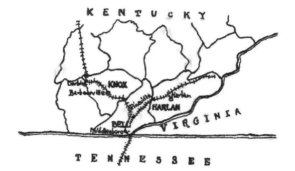

Ex-Pats Ink
Secret City USA

MURDER CREEK is a work of historical fiction. Apart from the actual people, events, and locales that figure in the narrative, all names, characters, places, and incidents are products of the author's imagination or are used fictitiously. Any resemblance to current events, current locales, or living persons is entirely coincidental.

MURDER CREEK by J. Kyle Johnson

Published by *Ex-Pats Ink, Secret City USA*
www.jkylejohnson.net

ISBN: 978-0-578-68458-1
Cover by Book Design Templates/Tanja Prokop

DEDICATION

For Robert "Papaw" Lasley
and all my Kentucky kin

Robert (Bob) Lasley, at left, with his brother Frank and their
mother Martha in Kettle Island, Bell Co., Ky., ca. 1916

FOREWORD

I labored in contented obscurity
to build an unadorned cabin
upon a rock of ages
(cleft for me).
Hour by laboring hour,
day after callused day,
hammering and hewing
log after ponderous log
'til at last it stood,
solid and sound,
imperfect, yet worthy,
a testament to quiet resolve.

MARCH 29, 2020 [JKJ]

CHAPTER 1

THE ELECTION

I don't mean to brag, but I got to say I was right proud of being elected sheriff of Bell County, Kentucky, in the fall of 1930, 'specially young as I was at the time and only being a deputy for two year before that. I run against Lovis Evans, the gap-tooth county coroner who had the backing of the biggest mining company in the county, Pioneer Coal, but the reason I was running that year was on account of I.D. Atkins, my boss and the sheriff before me, deciding to retire after getting shot by a bootlegger. He said twenty year was long enough to be sheriff anyway, but getting shot had made up his mind. Him and Virgil Helton, the Pineville city police chief, said they'd back me if I wanted to run, if for nothing else but to keep Lovis Evans and the coal company from winning, and they allowed as how they couldn't think of nobody better to put on the regular ballot in October than me.

I'd had my own run-ins with Lovis, but it weren't like we was special enemies nor nothing. I mean, there was that mess he got me into when I was investigating a killing at one of the Pioneer mines out at Kettle Island back when I.D. was laid up after the shooting. I couldn't get that weasel to sign off as coroner to say the miner's death was anything but a accident, which I'm sure the Pioneer Coal Company was grateful for, but it caused me no end of aggravation trying to investigate it as a murder.

It was that kind of a thing that got under my skin about Lovis running for sheriff. If he didn't want to do the job he already had, I couldn't stomach the idea of staying on and working for him as a deputy, even if he would let me after running against him, which I doubted. So that's how I decided to go ahead and throw my hat in the ring. It was as much to keep that weasel from becoming sheriff as it was me wanting the job for myself.

But then, right in the middle of the campaign, while I was out politicking all over the county at every cakewalk and revival I could find, damned if Lovis didn't up and quit! Just like that, he dropped out of the race and I was declared the winner. It was the damnedest thing anybody'd ever heard of according to I.D. and the chief, but that weren't the half of it. Turned out the reason Lovis dropped out was the town mayor offering him another job —and danged if it weren't Virgil's!

The way it come about was the chief had had a heart attack back at the end of the summer after helping me disarm and arrest a low-crawling snake by the name of Dewey Grimes at my house there in town. He ended up in the hospital and then at home before Doc Slusher said he could go back to work (*if* he took it easy and didn't get too excited, the doc said, which was like telling a goose not to honk and flap its wings). Mayor Hoskins, as it turned out, took that opportunity to start pressuring the city council to retire Virgil at the end of the year on account of his medical condition, and I'll be damned if they didn't go along with it and vote to push the chief out of office and hand his job over to Lovis come January. I can't prove nothing, but I also heard that the mayor was promised a stake in the Evans' family funeral business over in Middlesboro in return for the favor, but that could've just been a rumor somebody started down at the courthouse, likely the chief's gossipy daughter, Verda, at the switchboard.

Anyhow, Lovis won re-election to coroner, a surprise to nobody since he'd been coroner before that for two terms running. Now he was set to take over as city police chief too, and it didn't look like nobody could do nothing about it.

Maybe I ought've counted myself lucky and kept quiet, but I went to Judge Newsom after the election to ask if it was legal for Lovis to keep both them jobs—chief of police and county coroner, I mean.

"Politics is a low and slippery business, Sam," he told me in his office, "but justice nearly always wins out in the end if you can wait long enough for it."

Which I guess was just another way of saying *politics as usual* and telling me I ought to let sleeping dogs lay when it come to Lovis Evans.

***

Next chance I got, I made a point of finding Virgil in his office at the Pineville Police Station on the other side of the courthouse from the Sheriff's Office. Like usual, he was reared back in his big swivel chair, his belly pooched out like he'd swallered the ham hock with the beans.

I set down across from him in one of the office chairs, suddenly aware of how old and wore out he looked now, 'specially round the eyes. The hair across the top of his head was getting so thin he could've combed it with a rake.

I'd come to pay my respects and to ask him what he had in mind to do after he retired at the end of the year, being careful not to mention how it come about.

"How you doin' these days, Chief?" I started out, and that was all it took to set him off.

First he said he didn't know why he was coming into the office these days anyway, then he told me he didn't give two shits and bet me Lovis Evans wouldn't last six months if he lasted a day.

"This ain't like being coroner," he told me. "You cain't just wait 'til somebody dies and then show up."

He calmed down some after that, grabbed the peach can off the window sill behind him and spit t'baccer juice into it while I nodded and agreed with him, saying something along the lines of "Ain't that the truth" or "That's for dang shore," but I forget exactly what now.

After he got that off his chest, he put his spit can back on the sill and told me, "It ain't like I weren't thinking 'bout retiring before that peckerhead mayor stabbed me in the back, you know, Sam. I been thinking maybe it's time I was leaving here anyhow."

"Leave?" I asked, surprised to find out he had any idea of moving out of Pineville after all them years.

He chuckled. "Well, don't look at me like I said I was leaving here for France. I'm only thinking about moving across the river—maybe out to Fourmile."

"Fourmile?" I asked.

"Yep, had my eye on a little farm out yonder for some time now," he answered, reaching for his can again.

"That's where Livie's pa's place is," I reminded him, secretly wondering if there was something she ain't told me.

"Your girl," he answered. "That's right. Red Brock's place is just up the road from the one I'm looking at, ain't it. It's the Clayburn farm, but you need to keep that to yourself for the time being."

"You mean to buy Floyd and Alvey's place?" I asked after telling him I wouldn't tell nobody.

"I doubt they'd give it to me for nothing," he laughed.

"I didn't know it was up for sale."

"It ain't, but Floyd told me him and his brother was having a hard time making ends meet since I ain't had much call to use 'em as officers—not since the Fourth of July parade and then when I paid 'em to help you back in the summer was the last time—so I got to thinking maybe I'd swap with 'em."

"Swap?"

"Their place for mine," he told me, but listen, like I said, this ain't a done deal yet."

I was dumbstruck.

"How you gonna keep up a farm on your own?" I asked him, thinking about his heart attack that summer, but then, I didn't want him to think that's what I was thinking. "I mean, if Floyd and Alvey can't make a go of it, how're you expecting to?"

"I ain't interested in farming. I told 'em they was welcome to grow some corn or whatever they wanted out there and sell it. I'm only wanting some peace and quiet, and, who knows, maybe I'll get lucky and kill two birds with one stone."

"What birds?" I asked.

"*Love* birds," he told me, grinning like a cat. "Maybe if Alvey and Verda take a liking to one another, he'll take her off my hands for me."

"Verda know what you're up to?" I asked him.

"Hell, I gotta find *somebody* to take her off my hands, don't I? And they ain't been that many takers so far."

"You know what, Chief?" I said, thinking he might have better luck holding a auction for her out on the court-house steps.

"What's that, Sam?"

"This place ain't gonna be the same without you."

"It sure as hell ain't!" he grinned, reaching for his spit can again.

CHAPTER 2

NEWPORT

"You got some nerve showing up here," I told my sister's bum boyfriend Billy Wade Garrett the night he showed up out of nowhere while I was working at the 345 Club.

Here he was back in Newport again looking for Jonetta, and I felt like spitting in his eye. He'd been gone for I don't know how long, maybe three or four months since the summer him and his brother Sam was here and nary a word to my sister—not even a phone call to let her know if he was alive or dead—and now he'd slithered back into town looking for her.

"She don't want nothing more to do with you," I told him, but he only sneered like always.

I was holding a tray of drinks in front of me and had turned away to take it into the poker room when he grabbed me by the arm like I'd seen him do my sister, causing me me to spill the whole tray. It was all I could do to keep the bottles and glasses from crashing to the floor.

But it got Vince's attention behind the bar and he come out with a blackjack, holding it down by his leg, but where Billy could see it.

"You just bought yourself a round of drinks, fella," Vince told him as he slapped the balled end against his thigh.

Billy eyed Vincent like he was measuring his chances of taking him, which I could've told him was slim to none. I'd seen the barman take on two fellas at once and come out on top, throwing them out in the street on their backsides. Only other man I ever knowed to be as tough was Rocky Carbone, the one we called "Turk" back before he turned out to be a G-Man working undercover for the government and had to leave town after Jo tried to stab him, but that's another story.

I guess Billy figured the odds was against him, because he pulled a wad of cash out his pocket, which was something different for him from the last time I seen him. He peeled off two fivers and slapped them down on the bar.

"That's better," Vince told him. "Now run along home like a good little boy before youse has to be carried out."

Billy got red in the face and turned to leave, but not before pointing his finger in my face to say, "Tell her this is her last chance, sis. I'm leaving here with or without her."

"Ha," I said, laughing in his face, "some chance!"

He give me a wicked look but walked out all the same.

While Vince refilled my tray, he asked if Billy was talking about my sister.

When I told him he was, he laughed. "Ain't that kinda like a hyena taking on a female lion?"

***

At first I thought I wouldn't even tell Jo that Billy had come looking for her, but then I decided I ought to at least warn her he was in town. I couldn't leave the club in the middle of my shift, so I went looking for Gabriel to see if he'd do it for me.

Like usual, I found the spindly old colored man in the back of the club with the storehouse of the club's liquor and beer. He was setting in his rocking chair between two barrels of bourbon whisky, his eyes closed, waiting on Vince or maybe even Mister Albers to order a couple of crates or a barrel for the front. How a man that age could wheel them heavy loads to the front was beyond me, but from what I heard, he'd been doing it ever since the place opened.

"Now what kin ol' Gabriel do for you this evenin', Miss Jewel?" he asked me when I woke him up.

"You remember that man who come here bothering Miss Jonetta back in the summer?" I asked him.

He grinned. "You mean the one left out of here running like a scare't house cat when I got after him with my axe handle?"

"That's the one," I smiled.

"What's that polecat up to now?" Gabriel asked me. "He been bothering your sister again?"

"Not yet, but he's back in town. I seen him here tonight, and I'm hoping you can help me get a message to her before he finds out where she's at."

"Anything for you or yore sister, Miss Jewel," he smiled, showing two big rows of teeth the color of his wrinkled old skin.

What Billy Wade didn't know was Jo wasn't working the 345 Club no more. She was working a new club that was also being run by our boss, Louis Albers. The York Club was a "night house" over on York Avenue that Mister Albers bought from a man named Burk. Rumor had it Mister Burk had no thoughts of selling the place 'til he got a visit from Mister Albers' "business associates" from Cleveland. Whatever way it happened, Mister Albers took over the place and put in a bust-out joint downstairs for gambling and drinking while letting the working ladies stay on upstairs.

Jo don't have nothing to do with that part of it, though. Mister Albers said he wanted her to work downstairs, bringing in customers with her looks.

"They can do whatever they want upstairs," he told her, "once you get 'em good and liquored up."

That's her job, getting men to spend their pay on the way back home from their day jobs in Cincinnati. Course, it means she has to work the evening shift, but she always did like sleeping in, and it means more money and better tips.

So, anyhow, I asked Gabriel to carry a message to her over on York when he went to check on the store of beer and whisky there. It was the quickest way I could warn her in case Billy somehow found out where she was and beat me to it before I got off my shift.

***

I waited up late that night with the landlady's car in the parlor of our boarding house.

"What're you doing up?" Jo asked when she come in from work.

"Did Gabriel find you?" I asked her.

"Yes, and I 'preciate the warning, honey, but really there's no need. I ain't worried about Billy Wade."

"What if he finds out where you're working now? Or comes looking for you here? He knows where we live."

"I can handle Billy," she answered with a fake smile, "and besides, he knows who I work for now. He won't dare cross Louis."

"Mister Albers didn't do much to help you the last time Billy come looking for you," I reminded her.

"Why can't you call him 'Louis' like he told us to? You're the only one calls him 'Mister' Albers now. Even old Gabriel calls him 'Mister Louis'."

"I don't remember you two being on such friendly terms after he give you up to that Cincinnati bootlegger and almost got you killed."

"He explained all that," she answered. "He had no choice."

"No choice but throw you to the wolves," I told her.

"Quit your frettin' and go on to bed, will you? It's late and we're both tired."

"Just promise me you'll keep a lookout for him, alright?"

"You and Gabriel are all the lookouts I need, Jewel," she smiled. "Now promise me you won't worry."

But I did worry. I watched over my shoulder for Billy Wade the better part of a month and even give some thought to going to Mister Albers about him, except I knew Jo would throw a fit if I did. And in spite of the fact it's been weeks since I last seen him in Newport, I still worry Billy will show up again one day looking for my sister.

CHAPTER 3

THE CLAYBURN BROTHERS

I went back to the Sheriff's Office after my talk with the chief and got to thinking about what he'd told me about the Clayburn brothers—swapping houses, I mean, not the part about trying to unload Verda on Alvey. I'd been holding down two jobs for some time as acting sheriff after I.D. got shot, and now I was thinking about a kind of "swap" of my own. I could use a deputy and Floyd would make a good one. Him and his brother Alvey had both been working for Virgil as sworn officers from time to time, like when they helped me back in the summer after I tried and failed to shut down Dewey Grimes' bootlegging and gambling operation at Pickerin Pond, and I thought maybe I could hire Floyd for the Sheriff's Office before Virgil retired and that way avoid any chance of Lovis Evans getting wind of me "stealing" officers from under his nose. I mean, if Floyd and Alvey figured on moving into town and leaving their farm, they'd be needing jobs and I might not get the chance if I waited 'til January.

Floyd was a good bit older'n me. He fought in that big war over there in Europe and come back home to find out his pa had passed while he was gone, leaving Alvey to take care of the place on his own. Floyd tried to build the farm back up to where they could make a living off it, but everybody knowed the land out there was too poor to grow nothing but corn for whisky by then, and them boys weren't in that line of work so far as anybody knowed.

I got to know the both of them when they helped me and Jack Grimes bury his poor little sister Sadie and her baby up in Pickerin Hollow, and I liked them both, but it was Floyd I wanted to hire on account of I knowed he was a good man to have on my side in a tight spot. Alvey's a good feller and all, but he ain't got the same training and gumption of his brother. Problem was, I weren't the sheriff yet and wouldn't be 'til I got swore in by the judge in January. I didn't have the authority to hire nobody.

***

I figured talking to I.D. about it would be the best place to start, so I drove to the sheriff's house on my way home that evening from the courthouse and rung his doorbell.

"Evenin' Missus Atkins," I said when Mossie come to the door.

"Evenin', Deputy," she answered.

"The sheriff in?" I asked, knowing full well he hardly left the house anymore after the shooting.

"He is," she told me.

"Reckon I might talk to him for a minute, I mean, if he ain't already set down to his supper?"

She eyed me at first like she weren't real sure she wanted to let me in.

It weren't no wonder, though. Seem like every time I come to their house, it was on account of some trouble or other, and I weren't convinced she didn't blame me at least a little for her husband getting shot that night behind the courthouse. After all, it might never have happened if I'd met him there on time like I was supposed to.

"Can I see him for a minute?" I asked again.

"Who is it, Mossie?" I heard the sheriff holler, and that's when she moved away from the door to let me in.

"He's in the parlor," she said with a sigh. Like my ma, I.D. was spending most of his time in the parlor them days.

He put down the book he was reading and give me a welcoming smile when he seen me at the door.

"Come on in and have a seat, Sam."

I was took aback by how he'd changed in the short time since I seen him last. It seemed to me he'd shrunk to half his size somehow, though I knowed that couldn't be true.

"Sorry to be bothering you at home, Sheriff," I started out.

"Always glad to see you, Sam. What's on your mind?"

"Well," I started, then realized I hadn't thought out what I wanted to say and stopped. I was a little nervous about my idea of hiring a deputy.

"Deep subject," I.D. said with a slow grin.

"Yeah, well, uh," I started again, "I know I ain't been swore in yet and you're still sheriff and all 'til the end of the year, but, well, I was thinking maybe . . ."

"Better go on and spit it out before you choke on it, Sam, whatever it is," he interrupted me to say.

"Right," I answered, finally getting a grip on it. "Here's the thing. I wonder if you'd care to hire me a new deputy before you go out of office."

"Why?" he asked, raising a eyebrow.

"On account of I'm gonna need a deputy after I get swore in as sheriff and I've already got somebody in mind for it."

He frowned and shook his head. "You're gonna have to explain, Sam. I ain't following."

Which is what I.D. always said whenever he suspected I had something up my sleeve, so I went on to tell him where I'd got the idea from in the first place—leaving out the part where Virgil said he was thinking of swapping houses with the Clayburn brothers—and told him it was Floyd I had in mind for the job.

"You'll need a deputy, that's for certain, and I don't doubt Floyd Clayburn would make a good one, but there's just one problem with that plan," he answered, tilting his head to one side, "Where you gonna get the money to pay a deputy?"

"What?" I asked.

It was the one thing that hadn't entered into my thinking 'til right that minute.

"They ain't money in the budget to pay for nobody but you and me this year, Sam," he told me."I thought you knowed that."

I looked at the floor, grimaced, and scratched the back of my neck.

"Course, I might be convinced to resign a month or two early," he told me.

I looked up, surprised.

"Resign?"

"You're already swore in as acting sheriff," he told me. "No reason I can't resign right now that I know of. Ain't got nothing to gain by staying on 'til January, I don't think, but they's just one other thing."

"What's that?" I asked.

"You talked to Floyd yet?"

"No," I answered, "I wanted to check with you first."

"I 'preciate that, Sam, but don't you think you ought to know if he's interested in the job before I take the step of resigning?"

"You know, Sheriff," I told him for the first time since he got shot, "this job ain't easy as it looked when you was doing it."

"I know, son," he smiled, "I know."

***

I picked up the handset to the telephone first thing the next morning when I got back in the Sheriff's Office. When Verda, the chief's daughter, answered the switchboard, I started to tell her to get the Clayburn brothers on the line for me but never got the chance.

"When is it you and Livie are planning to tie the knot?" she asked before I could get in a word.

"What?" I asked.

"If Livie's looking for a bridesmaid, tell her I'm available," she told me.

"Look, Verda," I said, "I ain't got nothing to do with that. You'll have to ask her about that yourself."

"Well, if it's gonna be on Christmas Day like I heard, she'll have a devil of time getting a bridesmaid. I never heard of nobody getting married on Christmas Day before."

"Listen, Verda," I said, trying to get her back on the call I wanted to make, but it didn't take.

"Who's your best man?" she asked, hardly taking a breath. "You ain't expecting Billy Wade to show up, I don't wonder. You wouldn't want him standing up for you anyway, not the way he run off like he done with that Jezebel gypsy woman, whatever her name was."

She was talking about Jonetta, my brother Billy's *Melungeon* woman out of Wasioto, just outside Pineville. Her and Tick—that's the nickname he got from following me around so close when we was kids—they'd run off together that past summer to Newport, a town they call "Sin City" this side of the river from Cincinnati, which gives you some idea the kind of things that go on there. Then he got shot and run off from there to Cleveland without Jonetta. I hadn't heard a word from neither one of them since, though Colvin Schilder, the fed'ral agent I got to know from when I chased Tick up to Newport, told me later he'd hooked up with some crime gang there called the "Black Hand," whatever that is. All I know is, trouble attracted my brother like honey attracts bears.

"Look here, Verda," I finally said, "we ain't settled on none of that yet, so I just need you to ring up the Clayburn brothers' farm for me right now, alright?"

"No need to bite my head off, Sam," she huffed. "I was just asking."

"I'm sorry, Verda," I told her, "but I got official business that needs taking care of."

Me and her was too close in age was the problem. She wouldn't go on like that with I.D.

"Well, alright," she pouted, then finally made the connection for me and got off the line with a little *click* that let me know she weren't listening in on me.

I was hoping it would be Floyd who answered, but instead it was Alvey.

"Who's this?" he asked me even though I figured Verda had to've told him.

"This is Sam Garrett in the Sheriff's Office," I said. "Is Floyd about?"

"He's out in the barn."

"Tell him I'm calling from the courthouse and on my way out there to see him, will ya?"

The line went quiet of a sudden and I wondered if we'd got cut off.

"Alvey?" I said with a finger over the switchhook.

I was about to tap it twice for Verda when he come back on the line all out of breath.

"Floyd's out in the barn, Sheriff," he told me. "Said he cain't come to the telephone right now. He's up under the truck, working on the brakes."

From the sound of it, he'd run all the way out and back.

"Just tell him I'm on my way out there this morning," I repeated.

"Alright, Sheriff," Alvey said, then hung up without asking me why.

Anyhow, I figured to drive out and talk to Floyd about coming over to the Sheriff's Office to work for me. Like I say, Alvey's a good feller, but there weren't nobody I could think of better than Floyd—if he'd have the job.

When I got to their farm about a hour later, Alvey was waiting for me, setting in one of two cane bottom chairs out on the porch.

"Floyd told me to come out here and wait on you while he got cleaned up," he said, and I wondered how long he'd been setting out there in the cold morning air.

He got up and took a step towards the door but stopped like he forgot something and went back for the chair he'd been setting in. I opened the door and held it for him while he carried the chair inside, then followed him through the house to a near-empty kitchen at the back.

In the middle of the floor was a rough-hewed table, two cane-bottom chairs, and nothing else. Not another stick of furniture. There was a sink and a potbellied stove over to one side, but if they had a fire going, it weren't doing much to knock off the chill.

Floyd was bent over the sink washing his hands. He was up to his elbows in a pan of water, scrubbing away with a bar of lye soap.

"Sheriff's here, Floyd," Alvey announced as he slid the chair he brung in with him under the table and set down.

"I can see that, Alvey," his brother answered, turning his head towards me. "We're fixin' to have a bite to eat, Sheriff," he said, "if'n you're hungry."

I glanced at the table. In the middle was a roll of baloney, a block of crusty cheese, a raw onion, and three or four slices of bread.

"It's a dog's breakfast," Floyd said as he stood up and dried his hands on a greasy looking towel, "but like I say, if'n you're hungry . . ."

"I done et," I told him, eyeing the sickly color of the baloney.

Floyd set down across from his brother and picked up a bone-handled knife.

"Virgil told me you might be in need of a job," I said.

"That's true enough," Floyd answered as he sliced off two thick pieces of the baloney. "What little we been able to make working for the city ain't hardly enough to keep body and soul together."

Alvey slid his plate across to Floyd, who picked up one of the baloney slices between the knife's blade and his thumb and laid in on Alvey's slice of bread. Then he cut off two hunks of cheese—one for hisself and one for his brother—and slid Alvey's plate back across to him without a word.

"Well, if you're interested," I said, watching all this as I stood there between them, "I'm looking for a deputy to take my place in the Sheriff's Office."

"Where *you* goin'?" Alvey asked as he made hisself a sandwich of the fixin's.

"He ain't going nowhere, Alvey," Floyd told his brother before turning to me to ask, "When do I start?"

It caught me off guard.

"Ain't you got no questions?" I asked him, raising my eyebrows with surprise.

"When do I get paid?"

"Uh, well," I stammered.

Floyd stopped mid-bite to give me a wary look. Even Alvey looked up.

"Well, look," I said. "I only come out here today to find out if you was interested. I'll have to get back to you on the rest of it."

Floyd raised his chin and studied my face for a second, then nodded.

"Alright," he said. "You'll let me know?"

"I will," I promised, offering him my hand on it.

"Alright," he answered as we shook on the deal. "It ain't like I got any better offer right now."

I turned and left the house with a smile on my face. Now all I had to do was let Sheriff Atkins know.

But when I got back into Pineville from Fourmile, I decided to tell Virgil first and drove straight to his house there in town. It was on the way to the courthouse, so I figured if I didn't catch him there, I'd find him at the police station. I'd talk with I.D. next chance I got.

***

The chief's wife Alma answered the door when I knocked. She looked frazzled and was patting up her hair on one side where it had fell down from on top. She tried to catch a couple of straggling locks and put them back in place but give up on it when she seen who it was.

"Morning, Missus Helton," I smiled, "sorry to be bothering you this early, but I was hoping to catch Virgil if he's here."

She smiled back but looked puzzled.

"Mornin', Deputy," she answered, "but ain't he at the courthouse?"

"I don't know," I told her. "I been out in the county this morning and thought I'd drive by here and check first is all."

"He left out of here his regular time," she told me, frowning.

"Well, yes ma'am," I answered, "I 'spect he's there now. Didn't mean to worry you none."

We said our polite goodbyes and I drove on to the courthouse, parked out front, and walked inside to the police station. Parnell was setting at Virgil's desk and jumped up when I come in.

"Where's the chief?" I asked him.

"Ain't seen him today," the jailer answered, looking squeamish about me catching him playing at being the chief.

"That's alright," I told him. "I'll catch him later."

I left shaking my head and smiling to myself about Parnell thinking he could take liberties with the chief's office now that he was leaving.

I walked towards the Sheriff's Office at the other end of the courthouse, looking in at Verda on the switchboard as I passed by. She seemed busy, so instead of stopping to ask where her daddy was, I went to my office to call her.

Once there, I picked up the handset and clicked the switch a couple of times. I played with the twisted wires while I waited for her to answer.

"Switchboard," Verda said when she clicked in.

"You got any idea where your daddy, I mean, the chief's at? I stopped by the house, but your ma said he ought to be here."

"He's hiding out at the diner," she told me. "You want me to call over there?"

"Hiding out?" I asked, regretting it almost as soon as I said it.

"On account of Ma's been on the warpath lately," she went on. "He ain't never home on time no more, and when he does come in, he wants her to stop whatever she's doing and fix him something to eat. She's got fed up with it and told him he could just start eating at the diner if he couldn't be bothered to be home on time or at least let her know when he *would* be home, and if all he wanted was pie and coffee anyhow, he could just—"

I cut her off.

"Look here, Verda," I said. "When you do see your pa, just tell him to call me, okay?"

"Well, okay, *Sheriff*," she complained, "you don't got to bite my head off."

"Just tell him, alright?" I asked, polite as I could manage.

"Okay, then, I will," she pouted, unplugging herself from the line with a quick *pop* instead of the usual soft click.

But no sooner had I hung up when she buzzed me back again.

Picking up, I snipped, "What is it now, Verda?"

"It's that gover'ment man," she told me, still in a snit.

"Gover'ment man?" I asked.

"The one in Cincinnati," she said. "You know."

"Agent Schilder?" I asked, but she'd already popped off the line by then.

"Sam?" Schilder said from his end.

"Hello, Col," I answered.

"I understand congratulations are in order."

"How's that?" I asked.

"Seems like only yesterday we first met on your mother's front porch," he laughed, "and now here you are the high sheriff of Bell County!"

"Thanks, Col," I answered, "but it ain't official 'til the first of the year. How'd you hear about it?"

"Word gets around."

"It ain't hardly sunk in on me yet," I confessed.

"Give it time," he told me. "It's been a year since I took over as special agent in charge here, and some days I'm still trying to get my bearings."

"Well, I 'preciate you calling me," I said—and I meant it.

"I hate to bring this up at the same time, Sam, but it's not the only reason I called you today."

"How's that?" I asked, feeling a little disappointed that it weren't.

"Well, if you'll recall, I promised to let you know if I heard anything more about your brother."

Oh, hell, here it comes, I thought and braced myself for the bad news.

"He's left Cleveland."

"When?" I asked, wondering if he was headed my way.

"We don't know for sure—a month ago, maybe more. He was spotted by one of my men in Newport again, but I didn't learn of it until he'd already left town."

"Left for where?" I asked but not sure I wanted to know.

"Our best information is he's in Harlan County."

"Harlan County?"

"Best we can tell. Seems he's working for Baldwin-Felts down there. You know, the detective agency."

"Is that for sure?" I asked him.

"Can't say for certain, but we have had a report from there."

"Report?" I asked. "What kind of report?"

"The federal government's worried about strikes across the region and the Bureau—Mister Hoover, that is —wants us to keep track of where the Baldwin-Felts outfit is sending their detectives."

"You got a BOI man in Harlan?" I asked.

"No."

"Then who told you my brother's there?"

"I can't tell you that, Sam."

"Why not?"

"Look," he said, making it clear to me he weren't going to answer the question, "I feel bad about what happened to your brother—getting shot during one of our operations here, I mean—but I'm trying to keep my word, that's all. Maybe you should go to Harlan and see for yourself."

"I s'pect I'll have to," I answered, and then, of all things, I ended up thanking him for letting me know.

"Well, anyway," he said, "congratulations on winning the election."

"Thanks for calling," I said again, and we hung up.

I don't know what he was thinking, but I didn't much like the way he was throwing it my lap like Tick was my responsibility. Besides, it was one thing when my brother was five hundred miles away, but if what Col said was true, he was right here at my back door again.

***

After I got off the phone with Special Agent Schilder, I decided to clear my head by walking over to the Continental Hotel cafe to look for Virgil myself. My reason for finding him had changed now that I had my brother to worry about again, but I figured the fresh air would do me good and at least I wouldn't have to answer the telephone again for a little while. Lord only knows what else might be going on that I didn't know about.

Before Schilder's call, I only wanted to talk to Virgil about Floyd Clayburn, but now I wanted to ask what he thought I ought to do about Tick. Even though it weren't no secret Virgil didn't care much for my brother, I knowed I could count on him to steer me right, that is if I caught him in the right frame of mind. Besides, Virgil was about the only one who knowed all about Tick running off to Newport that summer and how he ended up working for a bunch of gangsters in Cleveland after getting shot by the "King of the Bootleggers" in Cincinnati. At least with Virgil, I wouldn't have to explain why having my brother in the next county over was so unsettling for me.

When I passed by the switchboard office on my way out, Verda held up her hand and motioned for me to come in.

I didn't want to, but she still had her earpiece on and acted like it was important.

"Daddy's waitin' on you," she told me, unplugging herself from the call.

"Where?" I asked, thinking he might've come back to his office.

"Over at the diner," she answered, then frowned. "Ain't that what you said—you wanted me to find him for you?"

"Well, yeah," I told her, "but I never meant for you to go tracking him down."

"Well, that's what I done," she bristled.

"That's fine," I said, raising both my hands in the air like a prisoner as I went out towards the courthouse door.

I walked out down the sidewalk and then across Pine Street towards the hotel, but halfway there I spotted Floyd Clayburn of all people climbing out of his truck.

It was parked out front of Sizemore's Hardware on the corner of Kentucky Avenue, so I cut the corner of Pine and started down towards him at a clip, hoping to catch him before he went in.

"Floyd!" I hollered, causing him to pull up and stop. "I was just about to call you."

He couldn't know it, but seeing him there—right there between spotting him on the street and flagging him down —I'd decided to take the bull by the horns and swear him in as a deputy come hell or high water so I could go looking for my brother. Virgil would say I'd lost my mind and I.D. would likely warn me against it, but I'd made up my mind and was sticking to it.

"Can you start first thing in the morning?" I asked him after explaining I had some unexpected business come up in Harlan.

Both his eyebrows shot up but he nodded and answered right off.

"I reckon," he said.

"Then meet me in the Sheriff's Office when you're done here," I told him.

He nodded again. "I got supplies to pick up first, though."

"That's alright," I told him. "I'll be waiting."

Right then and there, I turned myself back around and headed towards the courthouse again, forgetting all about Virgil.

***

Floyd knowed his way around the courthouse, so he found me in the Sheriff's Office not a hour later. I deputized him using the same badge I'd used to deputize my brother back in the summer, before I knowed he was mixed up in gun-running and bootlegging with Henry Yeager, the Baldwin-Felts man. I'd come to wish I'd never done it and hoped deputizing Floyd would turn out better than that did, but unlike my brother, Floyd had proved hisself to me in the past, so I swore him in.

Afterward, I shook his hand and reminded him to be there first thing the next morning, as I had business in Harlan and might not show up again 'til later in the day.

Knowing Floyd, I didn't think he'd ask many questions, and I was right. Course, I weren't sure I could pay the man, but I'd just have to jump off that bridge when I come to it.

CHAPTER 4

THE ROAD TO DAMASCUS

After deputizing Floyd Clayburn earlier in the day and telling him to show up to the Sheriff's Office the next morning, I headed home at dinnertime to tell Ma about the call I'd got from Agent Schilder and let her know I planned to run over to Harlan in search of her wayward son.

I went in the kitchen soon as I got to the house, expecting to find her laboring over a hot stove but instead found her running around the room with a flyswatter, slapping at a fat housefly that was moving faster than she could. She'd just missed catching it on the door of the icebox when I walked in.

"Want me to get my pistol?" I laughed.

"Very funny," she said as she chased it to the edge of the kitchen table, where she slapped at it and missed again.

The noisy fly lifted off and swerved towards the sink, but this time she didn't give chase. Instead, she handed the swatter to me. I took two long steps forward and nailed the buzzard as it landed.

"No mercy," I said, holding the swatter up to show her the splattered remains.

"That varmint's been pestering me all morning," she said, taking a deep breath. "I been chasing it all over the house."

"I know the feeling," I said as I carried it over to the garbage can to scrape it off.

"Go on and get washed up," she told me. "I'll have your dinner on the table here in a minute, now that dang fly's gone."

"No cussin' in the house, Ma," I teased her as I laid the swatter back on top of the icebox. "Ain't that what you tell me?"

"Oh, hush," she said, smoothing her hair back from her face before tying her apron around her waist.

"They's something I need to talk to you about," I told her as I went to the sink to wash my hands.

While I talked, Ma cooked, listening through to the end before saying anything.

When she did, it was, "Well, if Colvin says he's in Harlan, then I suppose you'd better go find out," but she didn't sound any more convinced than I was, I didn't think.

Like me, maybe she dreaded finding out. I knowed Ma held onto a frayed thread of hope that my brother would straighten hisself out one day and come back home to stay. I can't say I had much faith that he would, but I did have faith in our ma, so if she wanted to keep hanging on to that last thread, I weren't going to be the one to snip it in two.

We ate our dinner in silence, each of us lost in our own thoughts, 'til it was time for me to go back to the court-house.

"You'll want breakfast early, then," Ma said when I got up to leave.

"Just coffee, Ma," I told her, knowing full well she'd get up to fix ham and eggs and make me coffee whether I wanted her to or not.

***

That next morning, after eating Ma's breakfast, I put a change of clothes in the trunk along with my jacket and service revolver and headed on over to the courthouse. I was hoping Floyd would be there already so that I could get him settled in the Sheriff's Office and be on my way. It would take me a good hour or more of solid driving to get to Harlan, and that's if the road was passable this time of year. They was a new road being built up across Pine Mountain to the southeast, but I couldn't be sure how much of that was finished, so I planned to take the way I already knowed, which was out past Jenson Creek, then to Stoney Fork, and finally up and over the old logging road down into Harlan. It was steep as a mule's face but passable this time of the year.

When I got to the courthouse, I seen that Floyd was parked out front already, so I pulled in beside him instead of driving 'round back like usual.

"Glad you're here," I told him as we both got out of our vehicles and shook hands.

"I'll be getting me a uniform shirt soon as I get paid," he told me as we walked inside.

I took his measure as we walked down the hall and realized we was near the same height, though I probably had twenty pounds on him.

"I got a extry one hanging in the back of the office you can wear," I told him, "if'n it'll fit ya."

"Thankee, Sheriff," he said when we got to the door.

"You can keep it. I won't be needing it after I get swore in."

"I'll pay you back," he offered.

"No need," I told him as I opened up.

Inside, I pointed to the deputy's desk in the front room.

"Thatn's your'n," I told him, "but you can use mine to make telephone calls and the like whenever I'm not here. Toilet's in the back room."

He nodded and we stood there in the outer room looking at one another 'til I said, "Well, I'd best get started if I mean to get back from Harlan by dinnertime."

"I can take care of things here, Sheriff," Floyd answered.

"I know you can," I told him and turned to leave, "but I'll check in with you if I get the chance."

On the way back out to the car, I smiled and patted myself on the back for having the good luck to find a man like Floyd, but that good feeling passed as soon as I got on the road and I realized what a wild goose chase I was on.

***

By the time I got to the Cumberland River bridge, I come in a hair of turning around and going back into town, but then I got to thinking about Ma again and made the crossing onto the county road that followed Straight Creek to Jenson. Before I knowed it, I was half way to Stoney Fork and making good time. I give some thought to stopping there beside the road for a dipper of water from the spring, but I'm glad I didn't as it turned out. Just east of the Harlan County line, where it runs up the mountain, the road got rougher and meaner.

The roadbed on the Bell County side was pockmarked from logging trucks and buses that run roughshod over it every day, but it was in good shape compared to the potholes I run into on the Harlan County side. They'd been a big flood back in '27, I knowed, that washed out most of the roadbed, spilling it into the creek. They built it back, the runoff from the mountain made it so bad in places I had to slow to a crawl to roll through the ruts and around the gouges. It took me another hour to get to Harlan, glad the Model A didn't get mired up to the axle or break down along the way, but I got there in spite of the bad road.

It occurred to me after I hit town that I had no idea where to start looking for my brother. Harlan weren't no bigger than Pineville, but still it was like looking for a blacksnake in a coal shed, so I figured I might as well start where I'd tell anybody to start if they come looking for somebody in Pineville—the police station or the sheriff's office. They'd most likely be located in the courthouse, so that's where I went looking. I'd seen the clock tower when I drove down the mountain towards town, so I kept to the main road 'til I found the town square.

I parked out front of the courthouse, walked up the steps, went inside and asked the first person I seen to point me in the right direction. He was a man about my height but older like Floyd and had a shock of black hair that matched the two beetle brows above his eyes that made me think of the woolly worms Mammy watches to predict a bad winter. He was wearing a brown jacket and looked to be headed outside.

"Sheriff's Office is down there," he pointed after I asked him, "at the end of the hall."

"'Preciate it," I said, starting off to go that way.

"But the sheriff ain't there," he told me after I'd already took two or three steps in that direction.

I stopped and turned around. "How do you know?"

"On account of I'm the jailer," he grinned.

Now why couldn't you tell me that to start with? I wondered.

"Where can I find the sheriff, then?" I asked.

"At home," the jailer told me.

"When will he be back?" I asked.

"He won't."

"Well, then," I said, "maybe you can help me."

"Could be," he said, raising his bushy eyebrows. "What brings you to Harlan?"

"I come looking fer a feller," I told him.

"Little out of your jurisdiction, ain't ya?" he asked, looking down at my uniform shirt and badge.

I was starting to wonder if I'd made the right decision even coming to the courthouse.

"I'm just wanting to talk with him."

"What makes you think this feller's in Harlan?" he asked.

"Last place anybody knowed he was headed," I told him.

He pulled a pack of Lucky Strikes from his shirt pocket and slapped the bottom of the pack against the palm of his hand to coax out a cigarette.

"This feller you're lookin' fer," he said, bringing the cigarette to his lips, "what'd you say his name was?"

Suddenly, standing right there in the hallway, I decided not to tell him I was looking for my brother.

"Jack," I told him, "Jack Grimes."

To this day I don't know what made me say that other'n he weren't wearing a uniform. For all I knowed, he could've been lying about being the jailer for some reason or other.

"And what's he look like, this Grimes feller?" he asked me, lighting his smoke and taking a draw.

"He's a tow-headed feller," I answered, "'bout my age, maybe a year or two younger."

He studied me for a second as he let out the smoke, then tilted his head to one side and said, "Any younger and he'd still be in grammar school, wouldn't he?"

I felt the blood rush to my face.

"Now look-a-here," I told him, "you're talking to the next sheriff of Bell County, and I'd appreciate it if you'd take this a bit more serious."

"Don't get you're back up," he grinned. "I'm just funnin' ya." Then he smiled and asked, "Why you wearing a deputy's uniform?"

"I just got elected. Ain't been swore in yet."

"What happened to Sheriff Atkins?"

"Retiring."

"I guess that would explain why we ain't heard nothing from him in awhile. What's your name again?"

"Garrett," I told him.

"Garrett what?"

"Sam Garrett."

"Well, Sam Garrett," he said, stepping up to offer his hand, "I'm Lester Ball, but you can call me Les like ever'body else 'round here."

"So when's the sheriff due back?" I asked as we shook.

"He ain't due on account of he ain't planning on coming back."

"How do you know that?"

"On account of he's my brother."

"Your brother?"

"That's right," he answered. "My bother's the county sheriff."

"The sheriff's brother," I repeated, almost to myself.

"Not for much longer, though," he told me. "I mean he ain't gonna be the sheriff for much longer. Bell County ain't the only ones had elections this year, only Boyd lost his."

"Lost it?" I asked.

"More like it got stole out from under him."

"Cheated out of it?" I asked.

"Not exactly," he said, suddenly getting fidgety and looking around to see if anybody might be listening, "but we don't need to be talking about that here. You hungry?"

"What?"

"I was on my to get something to eat when I run into you."

"Oh," I said. "No, I done et this morning."

"How 'bout a cup of coffee then?" he said. "I'm buying."

I started to beg off then realized I didn't know where else to go from there.

"Alright," I said. "Where we goin'?"

"I was headed over to the *Corner Cafe*. We can walk it from here."

I followed him back out the front of the courthouse, where we cut across the wet grass and dead leaves to the street, then down the sidewalk towards the corner.

"Ain't you got no coat?" he asked on the way.

"In the trunk of my car," I answered.

"Well, it ain't far," he told me.

On the way, I asked him again about his brother.

"Boyd's quit coming in and they's only two deputies for the whole county," he told me, taking puffs from his cigarette as we walked, "but they're more beholding to J.H. now."

"Who's J.H.?"

"John Henry Blair. He's the one the 'sociation run agin Boyd in the election."

"What association?" I asked.

"Mine owners association," he told me, "They pretty much run this county nowadays."

"They the ones stole the election from your brother?"

He looked at me like I was a child.

"I don't know how these things work over in Bell County, son, but folks hereabouts votes the way the 'sociation tells 'em to. All but them that ain't beholding to the mines for a living, that is."

"That's a helluva way to run a county," I said, hoping I'd never see the day in Bell County when the mining companies run the vote.

"So, anyway," the jailer went on, "my brother got elected back when by sidlin' up to Judge Fuson and his party 'til the mine owners got together and formed the 'sociation here about two year ago and started buying votes and firing any miners that didn't vote the way they wanted."

"Why'd they want your brother out?" I asked.

"On account of Boyd's in favor of the union."

"What union?"

He give me that look again.

"The miners union," he said. "Course it ain't so much the union Boyd's for as it is them yaller dog contracts he's agin, the ones the companies make them men sign."

"What's a 'yellow dog' contract?" I asked.

"It's a oath they sign says they won't join the union—and if'n they do, they get blackballed and can't get a job nowhere in Harlan County after that."

I nodded, even though I'd never heard of such.

"I don't know about all that," I told him, "but I ain't got a lot good to say about mining companies myself."

"Had run-ins with 'em in Bell County, have ya? Well, if'n it's as bad there as it is here . . .," he said as he took the last draw off his smoke and flicked the butt out on the street.

"How bad is it?" I asked, thinking back to the "bull" Henry Yeager who worked for Pioneer Coal and led my brother astray.

"Bad 'nough that they's bringing in more of them damn gun thugs in here ever' day to bust heads and run anybody who supports the union out of the camps."

"Can they do that?"

"That's what I been telling ya. Hell, the 'sociation's even talked about calling the Army in here on 'em, like they done at Blair Mountain."

"You mean the *U.S.* Army?"

He laughed. "Is they another one hereabouts?"

"Where's Blair Mountain?" I asked.

"West Virginny," he told me. "Ain't you never heard of the coal wars in Matewan and Logan County, where they set the gun thugs and soldiers up agin the miners and unionists there?"

"No," I admitted.

He shook his head. "Son, your education is lacking some, I got to say."

"What happened?"

"Too much to tell," he answered as we got near the end of the street. "I just hope they don't send them army boys down on us like they did them. Paper said they brung in machine guns and killed more'n a hunnerd miners before it was all done. Shot and killed a police chief and a deputy right on the courthouse steps for tryin' to step in and stop it."

"The soldiers done that?" I asked, thinking about Floyd.

"Not them, necessarily," the jailer told me, "most likely some of them Baldwin-Felts bunch. We got them gun thugs swarming in here like flies now."

I come in a hair right then of asking him where I might start looking for my brother but decided against it. I weren't sure yet how much I could trust him.

"'Sociation calls 'em 'security police'," he went on, "hires 'em to protect their property, so they say."

"Is that all they're doing?" I asked, hoping that's all Tick had got hisself into.

"Like hell," he answered. "They's here to beat back the union, that's what, and this thing's building up to a regular war 'tween them and the miners, I tell you. If it keeps up, they'll be calling us bloody Harlan before it's over and done with."

The jailer stopped and pointed to a sign overhanging the sidewalk at the end of the block.

"Here we are," he told me.

I looked up and read the sign out loud.

"The *Corner Cafe*," I said, then laughed.

"What's funny?" he asked, looking confused.

"When you said we was going to the corner cafe, I thought . . . Oh, never mind."

***

We went inside the diner, the only two customers in the place, and set down together at a checkered cloth-covered table near the front. In about a minute, a tall raw-boned woman with a broad forehead come out from the kitchen through a swinging door, wiping her hands on her apron as she walked.

"That's Big Sal," the jailer whispered across the table. "She owns the place."

He set up straight and smiled when she reached us.

"Mornin', Sal!" he greeted her.

She stood with her hands on either side of her broad hips, looking down at him with steely gray eyes.

"Lester Ball," she said, "you got any idea what time of day it is? Breakfast is over and I ain't about to start cooking again for you nor nobody else 'til dinnertime."

She looked at me and the jailer looked sheepish.

"Sal," he said, smiling again, "this here's the new high sheriff of Bell County."

"You don't say," she said, raising her eyebrows. "Looks more like the new *boy* sheriff of Bell County, you ask me."

The jailer throwed his head back, slapped the table and laughed 'til I thought he'd lose his breath.

Big Sal never even blinked, just stood there with her hands on her wide hips, grinning down at me.

"Look here, Sal," the jailer said, sobering up, "I ain't had a bite to eat all day and neither's the sheriff."

I cut my eyes at him to say, *Don't be dragging me into this!*, but he wouldn't look at me.

"Stop it," Sally told him with a straight face. "You're breaking my heart."

"Ain't you got nothing for two hungry fellers?" Lester begged.

"Alright, alright," she said, holding her dishwater-chapped hands up in front of her. "I got some left-over biscuits and gravy I was fixin' to feed the cat, if it'll shut you up."

"Better'n nothin'," Lester told her, and she turned back towards the kitchen, plodding across the floor like a plow horse.

"Sal's good people," he told me when she was out of earshot. "She'll take care of a feller when nobody else will, but," he said, leaning across the table, "don't never let her hear you call her 'Big Sal'!"

While she was gone, Lester went on to tell me more about the troubles between the union and the coal companies. It was more than I ever hoped to know, but I listened. After all, I was learning things I'd never heard before, and, besides, I didn't have nowhere else to go.

"Like I was saying, it's them gun thugs causing most of the trouble 'round here now. This used to be a pretty fair place to live 'til the 'sociation started up and started bringing them Baldwin-Felts fellers in. But that was after the union convinced the men at the Lynch mine they'd be better off signing up with them to keep their wages up and the tonnage honest."

"And did they?" I asked.

"Did they what?"

"Sign up."

"Some did, but the mining companies fired ever' man-jack of 'em that they even suspected of sympathizing with the union, much less them that signed on. Fired 'em and brung in men from ever' damn where to replace 'em. Brung in piss poor white men and black fellers from all over the south and trainloads of furriners from God knows where-all, and most of 'em not even able to talk good English."

"Where's Lynch?" I asked, getting interested.

"Up at Black Mountain, end of the county just this side of Virginny," he answered. "It's the biggest mining camp in the county. They's four thousand miners out there, give or take, and twice that many women and chil'un. Got their own movie house, schools, hospital, police—hell, just about ever'thin'. It's owned by a big steel outfit out of Pittsburgh that's got more money than King Midas."

"They ain't that many miners in the whole of Bell County," I told him, wide-eyed.

"I don't wonder," he said, "but that's what brung the union in here. Even that John L. Lewis feller showed up here once. You likely seen his picture in the paper. He's that heavyset feller with them big bushy eyebrows."

I had to laugh, wondering how bushy a feller's eyebrows had to be to get Lester's notice.

I was caught up in the story by then and hardly noticed when Big Sal come back to the table with a pot of black coffee and a dinner plate full of butter biscuits with a bowl of thick gray gravy stuck in the middle.

"You can both eat off the same plate," she told us, dropping it down between us. "I ain't washing no more dishes."

Lester winked at me as she stepped to another table to get us two clean cups for the coffee. We watched as she poured.

"Thankee, Sal," Lester smiled up at her way too big.

"Eat up," she told him, ignoring his try at smoothing her feathers before she went back in the kitchen.

Turned out Big Sal's biscuits and gravy was some the best I ever eat, even left over, and by the time we finished the plate, I had a whole new appreciation for that woman.

I eat all I could hold and was wiping my chin on my sleeve when she come back for the plate.

"How much I owe you?"I asked as she refilled our coffee cups.

"Keep your money, honey," she told me."Like I said, I was fixin' to feed it to the cat anyhow."

"No wonder that cat's so damn fat!" Lester laughed across the table.

When she'd gone again, we each laid a dollar on the table and got up from our chairs.

"She always like that?" I asked the jailer.

"Sal's been through a lot," he told me as we went back out on the sidewalk. "Put up with a whoring husband 'til he finally got gutted in a knife fight with some woman's old man, then had to fight off the bank from taking the diner from her."

"I thought you said she owns it?"

"Does now," he said, taking out his pack of smokes.

"What happened?"

"Took 'em to court, that's what," he said, lighting up. "Judge Fuson give it all over to her once he heard the evidence. My brother Boyd was a big part of convincing him she was the real owner instead of Wix's people."

"Wix?" I asked as I took out the makings for my own smoke.

"Wix Howard," he answered, blowing smoke out into the cold morning air. "Man was useless as a broke pick."

We stopped on the sidewalk while I rolled one and lit up.

"Well, Sheriff," Lester said as clouds of smoke drifted away above our heads, "now that we're both fed and fat, what's yer plan for finding that boy you come lookin' fer?"

Now I was stuck in a tar baby of my own making.

"No telling where he's at," I said to avoid owning up to a lie, "but maybe you could put the word out? I mean, if anybody spots a—"

The jailer's eyebrows went up. "Son," he said, cutting me off. "They's thirty some mining camps in this county. You got any idea how many young fellers your age they are around here? And you're looking to find one driving a old truck? They's likely to a hunnerd or more!"

I took another draw and flipped my smoke out into the street, scattering firebrands like bits of burning coal. Lester throwed his down on the sidewalk, crushing it under his shoe.

"Well," I said, "you'll let me know, then, if you spot a boy and his dog drivin' a flatbed truck."

Lester grinned at me. "You got my promise on that, son. If I see a 'coon hound drivin' a flatbed truck, you'll be the first'n I call—right after the newspapers!"

I smiled at the joke but didn't say nothing back.

"Look, Sheriff," he said, getting serious again after having his fun, "I'd like to help, but they ain't much chance of me finding a boy that age, not with all the young fellers flooding in here from ever'where. It'd be like finding a dang needle in a haystack. But that don't mean I won't give 'er a try."

"I'd appreciate it, Les," I told him, starting to feel worse about lying to him in the first place.

"I'll get the word out best I can," he promised.

I avoided his eyes, instead looking across the square at the courthouse clock.

"Well," I said, "I'd best be gettin' back to Bell County."

"I'll let Boyd know you was here," he offered.

I nodded and stepped off the curb, heading back to the car.

**

Now that I'd already wasted half the day in Harlan, I figured it couldn't hurt to take a few minutes on my way back to stop in at Mammy's place in Stoney Fork. My thinking was to use the excuse of checking on Jack's sister Eugenia and the chil'un—the two littl'uns I'd left with Pauline for safekeeping after raiding Dewey Grimes' place in Pickerin Hollow—and find out if Jack had been back to see them since that night on the swinging bridge when I let him slip away. I still carried a axe to grind about the boy shooting his pa and getting away with it— in spite of the lie I told the Harlan County jailer—and wanted to hold him to account for it.

I went back the way I'd come but made better time now that I knowed where the worst parts of the road was. I slowed down where I had to, but mostly I sped on through, hugging the side of the mountain to avoid the worst ditches and potholes.

As usual, I pulled off the road at Mammy's and headed for the clear spring in the cleft of the rock overhanging the road. Like always, the beat-up tin dipper was there, stuck in between rocks behind the honeysuckle bush. I took a long drink and put the dipper back in its place before starting across the road to the bridge.

I don't know if it was the cool, clear water from the spring or the calming sound of the creek flowing below, but by the time I got half way across, a kind of peaceful quiet come over me and I become convinced things had worked out for the best in spite of the killing. Lord knows Eugenia and them two littl'uns was better off with Pauline and Mammy. I was still deep in my own thoughts when my aunt Pauline called to me from the path above.

"Well, skip to my loo my darlin'," she hollered as she walked down the hill followed by Roseasharon, the oldest of the two littl'uns.

The girl was carrying a tawny hen under one arm and had four yipping pups on her heels.

"Mammy *said* we'd have a visitor today," Pauline smiled as we got closer, "but she didn't say it'd be *you*."

"How you doing?" I asked her, noticing how she always looked the same—short curly hair cut close to her head, jeans rolled at the ankles, and a man's flannel shirt —always dressed for working 'round the house and out in the yard.

Nothing girly 'bout my Aunt Pauline, I thought, even though she was closer to my age than Ma's, her elder sister.

"We're doin' fine, Sam," she told me, taking my hand and patting it as she answered.

I pointed to the pups.

"Them can't be the same ones I brung out here back in the summer!"

"Follows her around ever'where she goes," she told me.

"Looks like you been feeding 'em pretty good," I said, "the young'un too."

"Spoiled rotten," Pauline smiled. "Ain't good for nothin' but chasin' chickens through the yard."

"The pups or the young'un?" I asked her.

"Both!" she laughed.

Then suddenly, in a fit of feathers, the hen flew out of the child's grasp and hit the ground running. The pups give chase and almost from habit I run after the hen, grabbing her up by the feet and carrying her upside down to keep her quiet.

"I see you ain't forgot *ever'thang* I learned ya," Pauline grinned, taking the hen off my hands as we started back up the path.

"How's Genia getting along?" I asked as we walked.

"Doing fine," she answered, "just fine. That girl's like a whole 'nother person now. You'd hardly know her."

"And how's the money holding out?" I asked her.

She stopped and looked at me, tilting her head to one side. The pups gathered 'round our feet, yipping and yapping at the hen.

"What money?" she asked.

"The money Jack brung you that evening," I told her, raising my voice to be heard over the pups, "that night I was here and run into the two of you on the bridge."

"Oh, that," Pauline answered, walking on, "hit's in a mason jar in the root cellar, hid in behind some rhubarb."

"The root cellar?"

"Or maybe the spring house," she said. "I ain't sure now. It's been awhile."

"Why ain't you using it to take a trip into town with Genia and them young'uns," I asked her, "maybe take 'em to the movies and get 'em some ice cream sodas or something?"

"Well, Sam," she told me, walking along with the chicken under her arm, "much as I 'preciate the boy bringing money for them chil'un, I don't know what he thought we was gonna spend it on. We got ever'thing we need right c'here. Plenty to eat what with the garden and what stores I put up for winter. Some of their clothes might need patching, but that ain't nothing. No need to waste that boy's money on new ones when the old ones will do."

Pauline stopped to toss the hen back inside the wire fence surrounding the chicken coop.

"Back where you belong," she said as it landed with a flop and run off towards the hen house. The pups stood watching from outside the fence, looking disappointed that they couldn't give chase.

"You too," she told the girl, reaching down to swat her on the backside and shoo her towards the house.

The pups followed 'til Roseasharon got to the first step, then run off on their own someplace up the hillside behind the spring house, and I give up talking about the money Jack left in a paper bag for them chil'un the night I run into him out on the bridge—before he run off to Harlan. He'd found it under his pa's shack and brung it there for Pauline to use, but I didn't feel like I could tell her how to spend it. I did think I might get Ma to have a talk with her about getting them some good shoes and pretty dresses, though.

We followed Roseasharon up the steps onto the porch, where she run straight to Mammy, who was setting out in her rocker as usual.

"How you feeling these days, Mammy?" I asked as Roseaharon scooted in beside her.

"Tolerable well," Mammy answered, her eyes smiling at me as she smoothed the child's wild hair.

"A might cool to be setting out here on the porch this mornin', ain't it?"

Just then, the screen door busted open and the other young'un come flying out nekkid as a jaybird.

She run between Pauline and me and headed off the porch. My aunt made a grab for her but missed, then Eugenia come out, hopped clean off the porch, caught the child by one arm at the bottom of the steps, and scooped her up by her bare bottom.

"Gettin' this young'un a bath is like wrestlin' a greased pig," she fussed as she carried the child back up on the porch. "Cain't turn my back fer a minute."

"Better get that child inside before she catches her death," Mammy cackled.

"And you," Genia said, pointing a finger at Roseaharon, "you're next."

"Been heating water on the stove all mornin'," Pauline told me. "Takes the both of us to hogtie them varmints and keep 'em in the washtub. I better get in there and help her before the water goes cold."

Pauline and Genia disappeared inside with the baby.

Mammy called to me when it got quiet on the porch again.

"Samuel Lee," she said, "come over here and set down a minute."

I dragged one of the cane-bottom chairs over while she helped the young'un climb down off the rocker and told her to go inside.

"Little pitchers got big ears," Mammy told me as she dug her snuff can from the folds of her skirt to take a dip.

I watched 'til she was done, noticing that the craggy lines of her face seemed deeper, the granny whiskers on her chin longer, and her graying hair—drawn tight into a bun at the back of her head—thinner since the last time I seen her. I wondered how much longer we'd have her with us and knowed I'd miss her like the dickens when she was gone.

"Had me a dream t'other night, Samuel," she said at last.

"What kind of a dream, Mammy?" I asked, thinking it might be one of her waking dreams, one of her *visions*.

"Pauline don't want me to tell it," Mammy answered, "but I think you ought to hear it."

"Maybe Pauline ought to let me be the judge," I smiled.

Mammy nodded, took a quick look behind me at the door, then said, "It was two catamounts, Sam, paint'ers the size of full-growed men."

I raised my eyebrows and waited while she used her spit cup.

"Well sir," she went on when she was done, "them two paint'ers, they was a'chasin' a wild-eyed buck down a mountain—down a huntin' trail that run right out of the woods and into town."

"What town?" I asked.

"Not one I ever seed before," Mammy told me.

"Alright," I said, "then what?"

She closed her eyes and raised her pointed chin, like she was seeing it again.

"That young buck, he was running scare't all through that town, up and down alleys, tryin' ever which a way he could to git them two wildcats off'n his tail. But they was runnin' for all they was worth too and gittin' closer and closer 'til they'd chased that buck right into a trap."

"A trap?" I asked, trying to figure out where this wild tale was going.

"And then one of them paint'ers reached out and grabbed hold the young buck's haunches, bringing it to the ground."

Mammy suddenly stopped, closed her mouth in a tight line, and opened her eyes.

From behind, I heard Pauline say, "Breakfast is on the table whenever you two git done talking foolishness out here," and turned to see her disapproving shadow standing behind the screen door, both arms crossed in front of her.

"It's alright," I answered her, laughing, "I ain't a'skair't!"

Mammy cackled.

"Well don't blame me if the food gets cold," Pauline scolded before going back inside.

"Reminds me of Ma," I told Mammy after she'd gone, then stood up to help her out of the rocker.

"You stayin'?" she asked me.

"No, ma'am," I told her. "I done et twic't today, and, besides that I got to get back into town."

I held Mammy's thin, brittle arm and helped her to the door.

"So what happened to the buck?" I asked as I opened it for her. "Did he get away?"

"No, son," she frowned. "Them catamounts killed that buck right there in that alley."

I thought about Mammy's tale all the way down the path to the creek and across the swinging bridge, but I couldn't make heads nor tails of it, and by the time I got back in the car, I'd put it out of my mind altogether because I had something else on my mind by then—my cousin Curtis.

***

Since it was on the way, I decided to stop off at my cousin Curtis' pole cabin on Jenson Creek to find out if he'd heard or seen anything of Jack Grimes since the last time I stopped by, which was way back before the election.

As I drove up the overgrowed wheel path through the woods, I spotted a thin trail of wood smoke coming from the chimney, letting me know he was likely t'home, so I pulled up to the porch, got out, and walked up the steps to the open door.

"Howdy, *me*-Sam," Curtis called out from inside, using the pet name he'd had for me since we was boys, but he sounded more wary of me now for some reason.

He was setting in front of his fireplace with his back to the door, using a poker to stoke a weak flame under a smoldering, scrawny carcass he'd skinned and skewered.

"What is that?" I asked him.

"Squirrel," he answered. "You hungry? They's enough for two here."

"No," I told him, "eat is about all I've done today, but I could use a little of your well water to cool off my engine."

There weren't nothing wrong with the engine, but it was all I could think of to explain why I'd showed up there of a sudden after all this time.

"H'ep yerself," he told me without turning around. "You know where it's at."

I stepped back outside and went 'round the side of the house to fill a bucket with water. The radiator didn't need it, but it made me feel less guilty for lying about it and give me some more time to think what I wanted to ask him before going back in. I left the bucket on the bottom step as I come back up on the porch.

The early light coming in through the open door barely lit the inside of the cabin, and the weak flame from the fireplace did little to warm it up. I walked in and stood across the table from my cousin, wrapping my arms around me to keep warm and thinking I should've got my jacket out and put it on.

"Sure you don't want none of this, *me*-Sam?" Curtis asked me again. "It ain't much," he went on. "Better'n nothin', though, and 'sides, I didn't even have to leave the house to hunt the critter down."

"What?" I asked.

"Yep, danged if he didn't walk right up on the porch this morning and practical beg me to shoot him. Stood right there at the door on his hind legs, lookin' in."

"That right?" I laughed.

"Didn't even have to git up out'n the chair—just reached over real slow for my rifle, aimed from the hip and *pow!* Easiest huntin' I ever done."

"Maybe you ought to try laying a pile of hickory nuts out there," I told him. "Might get you one like that ever' day."

"Ha! Now you're thinkin'!" he answered, his back still to me as he tended the squirrel.

That's when I decided to throw out the real reason I come by and see how he'd take it.

"Listen, *me*-Curt," I said, "since I happened by . . ."

He turned his head and cut me a sidelong look.

"*Happened by*, huh?" he said. "This here squirrel happened by too, didn't he? You ain't even set down yet, you know that? How 'bout you quit mealy-mouthing me, set your tail down, and tell me why you drove all the way out here—and don't tell me it was fer a bucket of goldern water."

Right then I was glad for the dim light in the cabin, so he couldn't see my face growing red from embarrassment.

"I come to ask you about Jack Grimes," I told him after setting down in the only other chair at the rickety table.

Curtis laughed. "Is that all? Hell, son, from the look on your face, I thought you'd come up here to tell me I was being arrested!"

I smiled a bit, then asked again. "You seen the boy, *me*-Curt?"

He narrowed his eyes. "I thought you'd give up on that notion."

"What notion is that?" I asked.

"The notion he ought to be jailed for what he done."

"I've thought better of it since then—letting him get away with it, I mean."

At that Curtis turned around to face me with the poker in his hand, waggling it in my direction.

"You mean you've thought better of it now that you're the sheriff," he said like a accusation.

"I ain't the sheriff yet," I reminded him, "and this ain't got nothing to do with that one way or t'other."

Curtis turned back to the fire.

"This is me you're talkin' to, *me*-Sam, remember?" he said, reaching out to test the cooked meat with his fingers. "The two of us is still veined and blooded, ain't we? Or is that badge gettin' in the way of you listening to me now?"

"Don't git your back up," I told him.

"I ain't got my back up," he declared, laying the poker down to pull a bit of stringy meat off the blackened carcass. "Maybe you're just fergettin' who it was got the boy into that mess in the first place. If you'll remember, we both talked him into taking you up Pickerin Holler just so's you could bust up his pa's bootlegging and gambling outfit, and you seen how that turned out fer 'im."

"I ain't forgot," I told him as he tested the heat of the meat on his tongue before taking it between his teeth to chew like jerky, "but there ain't no getting around him being the one burned down his pa's shack and most likely shooting him with that rusted .45 Dewey called 'Old Huldy'."

"Hit might never of happened if you hadn't decided to take them girls out of the house," he reminded me as he pulled a piece of gristle out of his teeth.

"I know that," I owned up, "but that girl was dying, and Lord only knows what all Dewey done to her and her sister."

"I ain't saying you done the wrong thing," Curtis admitted as he reached in for another bite. "I'm only saying it's what led to Dewey's killin', that's all."

"I never told the boy he ought to shoot his own pa and leave him for dead."

Curtis turned to face me, a piece of steaming meat in his fingers.

"Dewey Grimes got what he deserved, *me*-Sam," he told me. "You know it, I know it, and there's a end to it."

"That ain't what the law says," I answered.

"Whose law?" he asked, looking me in the eye. "Mine or your'n?"

"Now look here, *me*-Curt," I said. "I'm asking you straight out. If you know where the boy's at, you need to tell me."

"Huh," he grunted, "I ain't got to do no such a thang."

"That's it, then? You ain't gonna tell me?"

"What's done is done, Sam," he answered. "Let sleeping dogs lay."

With that, he raised hisself out of his chair, took up his crutch and started for the back door.

"Where you going?" I asked.

"I got some personal business out back," he told me, "so less'n you want to holler at me through the outhouse door, we're done talkin'."

CHAPTER 5

THE JUDGE

It was near dinnertime when I got back to Pineville from my cousin Curtis' place and pulled in behind the court-house. I parked in the gravel lot out back of the Sheriff's Office and walked in through the back door and down the hall.

The door to the outer office was open and Floyd Clay-burn was setting at the deputy's desk in the front room, reading the Pineville paper. I noticed he'd put on the uni-form shirt I'd offered him. It was a decent fit and I was glad for him to have it.

"Mornin', Floyd," I said as I walked in. "Anything im-portant come up while I was gone?"

He rubbed one eye with the back of his hand and cleared his throat before answering.

"Nothing I couldn't handle, Sheriff," he finally said.

I had to grin. I don't know how many times I'd an-swered the same way whenever I.D. come in asking me the same thing.

"The chief come by here a while ago, though," Floyd added. "Said you was looking for him?"

"I was," I answered.

"Seem like he was kinda surprised to see me here," Floyd added.

"That's why I was looking for him," I said, "to tell him I'd put you on as a deputy."

"Too late now, I reckon," Floyd pointed out.

"I reckon," I agreed. "He ask you anything about it?"

He shook his head. "No, just said tell you he might be back after dinner if you was still looking for him."

"Alright," I said, then went on through to my desk.

As I stood there rifling through some papers before setting down, it occurred to me Floyd might be wanting his dinner too.

"I got some catching up to do here if you want to take your dinner break," I called out to him.

"If it's all the same to you," he answered, "I'll stay here."

"Ain't you gonna eat nothing?" I asked.

"I left my dinner pail at the house," he told me, but after what I seen in his kitchen at the farm, I wondered if he was telling me the truth or maybe just didn't have nothing to put in a dinner pail.

I started to offer him money to eat on but didn't want to embarrass him, and I weren't planning on getting nothing at the diner or going home, so instead I told him to take the rest of the day off.

He hesitated at first, then asked if I was gonna need him to come in the next day.

"Tomorrow's Sunday," I reminded him

"No matter," he told me. "I can be here if you need me."

"I'll let you know," I answered. "Alvey's gonna need a hand with the farm, ain't he?"

He nodded, then got up from the desk and come to the door.

"They's just one thing," he said.

"What's that?" I asked, looking up.

"I was wondering when I might get paid—if'n it ain't to soon to ask."

"Oh," I answered at first, not letting on that I didn't know, then told him, "You'll get a week's pay next Saturday." *Even if I have to take it out of my own pocket,* I thought to myself.

Floyd nodded again and said, "They's just one other thing, Sheriff."

I cringed.

"What's that?" I asked, raising my brow.

"I just want to thankee."

"For what?"

"Ever'thing," he answered.

I smiled, a little embarrassed, and said, "See you Monday, then, Floyd."

"Monday, then, Sheriff," he said, giving me a quick two-fingered salute before turning to leave.

It was a world of difference having a feller like Floyd around, I thought.

***

After Floyd had gone, I picked up the telephone handset and tapped the switchhook for Verda.

A female voice answered, but it weren't Verda's.

"Who's this?" I asked.

"It's Lucybell, Sheriff."

"Oh, right," I said.

"Verda don't work Saturdays no more," she reminded me.

"I just forgot," I told her. "Listen, can you get Judge Newsom on the line for me?"

But there was no answer. I was reaching out, ready to hit the switchhook again, when she come back on.

"I found him, Sheriff," she told me. "He's at home having his dinner, like I thought."

"Oh," I said, surprised by the girl's giddy-up. If that'd been Verda, I'd have had to lead her around by the nose to find him for me.

"You're welcome, Sheriff," she said. "And congratulations, by the way."

"Congratulations?" I asked, wondering if Verda had been gossiping to her about me and Livie.

"On getting elected sheriff, of course," she answered with a giggle.

"Oh, right," I said, feeling a little foolish.

"I'll connect you now," she told me, and I heard the little *click* telling me she was off the line.

"Sam?" the judge said.

"Sorry to bother you while you're at dinner, Judge," I said, "but I was hoping to meet with you this afternoon, if you can do it."

"What's this about?" he asked.

I could tell he weren't happy.

"I'm sorry, Judge, but I need to ask you a question about the money."

"What money?" he asked.

"I.D.'s budget," I answered, "the county budget, I mean. I got a question about hiring a deputy."

"You only just got elected. Why don't you ask I.D. about that? He's still the sheriff, you know."

"I know," I said, starting to think it was a mistake for me to call him.

"Well, alright," he sighed. "Meet me in my office. Two o'clock . . . and no later."

"Thankee, Judge," I said, but he'd already hung up.

***

I'd hardly put down the phone when Chief Helton showed up at my door.

"Heard you was looking for me," he said. "Where you been all morning anyway?"

"Harlan," I told him.

"Harlan? What the hell you doing in Harlan?"

"I went looking for Dewey Grimes' boy."

It was the same lie I'd told the jailer, but now that I'd started down that path, I figured I might as well stick with it.

"The one I took the hogleg pistol off of outside the jailhouse after we throwed Dewey in jail?"

"That's the one," I told him. "I figure that's where he run off to after shooting his pa."

"What's that got to do with me?" he asked. "I ain't got a dog in that hunt."

"I know. That ain't why I was looking for you."

"Then why are we talking about it?"

"We *ain't* talking about it," I said, shaking my head.

"Then why am I here?" he asked.

I stared at him for a second before answering, getting my thoughts straight.

"On account of I wanted you to know I offered Floyd Clayburn a job as a sheriff's deputy."

"I know that already," he told me.

"I know you do *now*," I said.

"I don't know why you thought you needed to tell me," he said. "I reckon you can hire who you want."

"You don't care that I hired him out from under you, then?"

"No. Floyd's a good man, but he ain't worked for me in some time—him or his brother either one. You sure you got the money to pay him?"

"I'm meeting with the judge about that this afternoon," I said.

"Well, good luck with that," he told me. "The judge is tightfisted as a banker when it comes to the county's money."

"Meaning what?" I asked.

"Meaning he ain't likely to approve you bringing on a new deputy 'til I.D.'s off the payroll and you're swore in as sheriff."

***

By the time I got Virgil out of the office, it was dinner time and I had a headache pounding at my temples. I weren't much hungry but needed to lay down for a few minutes and close my eyes.

At the house, I found Ma asleep in her chair in the front parlor and realized I'd forgot to call and let her know I'd be coming. I near always let her know, but this time, what with running over to Harlan and back and try-ing to figure out how I was going to pay Floyd, I'd plumb forgot.

Her bible was open in her lap, but she'd nodded off, purring like a house cat.

"Ma," I whispered, shaking her by the shoulder

When she didn't wake up, I tried again, louder this time, and she opened her eyes.

She had a blank stare 'til she come to herself and asked, "Where's Billy?"

I figured she'd gone to sleep thinking about him.

"He ain't here, Ma," I told her.

"What time is it?" she asked, looking around, her voice hoarse with sleep.

"It ain't late," I told her.

"I'll have you something to eat here in a minute," she said, closing her bible to get up.

I said, "No, stay where you are. I only come home to lay down a minute before heading back to the courthouse. I got a meeting with the judge this afternoon."

"You cain't go all day without eating," she said.

"I had a bite over in Harlan this morning," I told her.

"Where's there to eat in Harlan?" she asked.

"They got diners there," I answered, then changed the subject. "We got any aspirins?"

"Upstairs," she said, starting to get up again, "in the medicine cabinet. I'll get you one."

"No," I told her, "I'll get it."

Out in the hall, before heading up, I slipped off my boots and left them on the bottom step, meaning to lay down for awhile after getting myself a aspirin, but next thing I knowed, I heard Ma pecking at my door.

"Sam?"

Her voice seemed a long way off, thin and distant like the call of a whip-poor-will. I opened my eyes and stared at the ceiling.

"Sam?" she called again, knocking louder.

"What is it, Ma?" I answered from the bed.

"Didn't you say you had a meeting at the courthouse this afternoon?"

I jumped up.

"What time is it?" I asked her at the door.

"Near two," she said as I rushed past her and down the stairs.

"Will you be home for supper tonight?" she called as I set down on the last step to pull on my boots.

"Most likely," I answered, then run headlong out the front door.

***

I cranked the Ford back to life and sped out to Pine Street, praying the whole way back to the courthouse that Judge Newsom hadn't got there ahead of me. I parked in front and rushed up the wide set of stairs from the vestibule to the second floor, taking them two at a time.

I trotted down the hall to my right, past the court and towards the judge's private office. As I reached for the doorknob, I heard his voice roll out over my head through the open transom.

"If he's not here in five minutes," he was telling somebody inside, "I'm heading home."

And when I opened the door and walked in, it was I.D. I found setting across from him at the desk.

I frowned and without thinking said, "How come you're here?"

But it was Judge Newsom who answered, raising a brow and narrowing his eyes at me.

"He's here at my invitation, Deputy. He's still sheriff, you know."

"Virgil called me," I.D. said, without the accusation in his voice that the judge was making.

"I only meant—" I started to say, but the judge cut me off.

"Have a seat," he told me, "I.D.'s already explained what you're up to."

I looked at the sheriff as I set down.

"Don't worry, Sam," he said, shaking his head.

I breathed a sigh of relief, but it turned out the judge weren't done with me yet.

"It's my understanding," he went on, fixing me with a hard look, "that you already promised a job to one of Virgil's officers?"

"Yes sir, Judge," I confessed.

"Floyd Clayburn's a good man," I.D. added, most likely for my benefit.

"That's fine," the judge went on, "but if you think I'm going to stand by and let I.D. here resign before you're sworn in as sheriff, then you've got another think coming. Don't you realize he'd be giving up two months' salary on your account?"

I slumped back in my chair, suddenly feeling lower than a egg-sucking dog.

"Well, no," I stammered, looking over at the sheriff, "if I'd a knowed that . . . I mean . . . I never would've . . ."

"I know you wouldn't," I.D. said.

"Regardless," Judge Newsom cut back in, "here's how we're going to handle this thing."

That's when he drug a thick ledger out from one corner of the desk and slid it under my nose.

"Know what this is?" he asked as he opened it to the front page.

"No sir," I answered, looking down, and for the next hour, him and the sheriff commenced to educate me in the ways of delinquent property taxes.

"So," the judge summed up after we'd gone through most of the book, "now you know how you're going to pay for that new deputy you went out and hired—that is, unless you've changed your mind."

I.D. felt sorry for me, I could tell, but he set quiet, waiting for a answer. Judge Newsom only stared.

I stood up from my chair, took up the ledger, and tucked it under my arm like I was fine with trying to collect back taxes from every recalcitrant land owner in the county.

"I'd best be getting started, then," I said, trying hard to smile.

"Good," the judge said, leaning back in his chair with his hands behind his head. "Then we have us a understandin'?"

I swallered hard and answered, "Yes sir, we do."

CHAPTER 6

PRODIGAL SONS

I'd had no luck finding my brother when I went over to Harlan County looking for him and now Ma was starting to ask me about it. She weren't pushing me to go back and find him nor nothing like that. It was just little things she'd say, like asking me if I'd heard from "Colvin" recent, meaning Agent Schilder at the Bureau, or if I thought maybe I ought to call the hospital in Harlan or the county sheriff to find out if a Billy Wade Garrett had been in a accident there anytime recent.

Course, I didn't let on that Schilder had already told me Tick was working as a Baldwin-Felts "bull" for the mine owners' association, but after a time I felt like I owed it to her to make some kind of effort. So the next Saturday, I took it upon myself to call Les Ball, the jailer, again.

Floyd was out running errands that morning and Verda didn't work Saturdays no more, so I shut my door and buzzed Lucybell at the switchboard.

"Yes, Sheriff?" she answered, perky as ever.

"Can you get the Harlan County Sheriff's Office for me?" I asked her.

"Are you going to be in your office?" she asked.

"Why?" I asked.

"This might take a minute."

"Sure, okay," I told her, "I'll be here."

"Do you only want the sheriff or is there somebody else you can talk to?" she asked me, thinking ahead.

"Anybody who'll answer," I told her.

I got up to go to the toilet, but she buzzed back even before I could get to the privy door.

"I have a Lester Ball on the line for you, Sheriff," she told me when I set back down and picked up.

"Is this the *boy sheriff* of Bell County?" Lester asked, laughing like a billygoat.

"How ya doing, Lester?" I greeted him, hoping Lucybell hadn't heard that.

"I'm slicker'n a minner's dick and sharper'n a miner's pick, son, how 'bout you!"

" 'Bout the same," I answered, shaking my head.

"You ever find that boy who lets his 'coon hound drive the truck?" he asked, still laughing.

"As a matter of fact, I'm looking for somebody else now," I told him, trying to backfill the hole I'd dug for myself about that.

"And who might that be?"

"It's one of them Baldwin-Felts fellers," I told him.

"Now what in the fiery world would you be looking for one of them sons-a-bitches fer?" he asked.

I struggled to come up with a reason but couldn't think of one off the top of my head. Instead, I said, "It's, uh, my . . . I mean . . . it's a relation of mine. I heard he might be there and thought maybe I ought to warn him what he's got hisself into after what you told me last time."

I shook my head and rolled my eyes at my own story, figuring he'd see straight through it.

"What's this feller's name?" he asked.

"Billy," I told him.

"Well, that ain't much help," he said with a *humpf.* "What's his *last* name?"

"Garrett," I answered, waiting for the other shoe to drop, but all he asked after that was, "Which camp's he in?"

"Which camp?" I asked, not understanding.

"It's like I told you when you was here before, they's thirty or forty mining camps in these hills and hollers. Which'n is it you think he's in?"

"I ain't got no idea," I admitted.

He pondered a second, then said, "Well, if'n he's a Baldwin-Felts man, he's most likely working for the 'sociation, and if'n he's working for the 'sociation, he'd most likely be up in Lynch. That's where they been puttin' most of 'em here lately."

"I ain't sure," I told him, thinking back to my conversation with Agent Schilder.

"Well, when'd he get here?"

"Maybe a month ago."

"They's been more'n a few of them fellers come through here in that time, I can tell you."

"Any chance of you finding him, then?" I asked, already losing hope.

"Nope," he answered me flat out, "but I'll keep a eye open. What's he look like?"

"A lot like me," I told him, "but freckled and got copper-colored hair. He's a couple years younger'n me, too."

I regretted saying it as soon as it come out of my mouth, but it was too late.

He belly laughed. "*Younger?* You mean he don't even shave yet?"

I knowed there'd be more and waited on it.

"Now, let me get this straight," the jailer said. "I'm writing it down here—copper hair, freckles, and peach fuzz. Is that about it? Shucks, man, if I cain't find him now, I just ain't trying!"

***

I hung up after talking to Lester that morning thinking there weren't a snowflake's chance in hell I'd be hearing from him again, but it weren't even a week 'til I did.

"How's things going over there in Bell County, Sheriff?" he asked as soon as Verda patched the call through. Then, without waiting for a answer, he said, "Listen, you know that feller you was looking fer? Not the Baldwin-Felts feller, the boy—the one that lets his dog drive his truck."

"What?" I asked. "You seen him?"

"I'll go you one better. I know where he's at."

"Where?" I asked.

"Cain't tell you that over the phone," he answered. "Any chance of you coming over here to see him?"

I was dumbfounded.

"When?" I finally asked.

"Tonight," he answered.

"Tonight?"

"You might want to hear what he's got to say."

"About what?" I asked.

"You'll find out when you get here," he told me.

I went quiet, trying to think, then asked, "What is it he's telling you?"

"*You're* the one looking fer *him*, remember?"

I couldn't argue the point.

"Where you wanting to meet?" I asked, too curious not to go find out.

"Just park where you done last time you was here. I'll find you."

"I'll be there soon as I can make it," I told him and hung up to call Ma to tell her to save my supper for me. After all, how long could it take to drive over there and back and find out what this was about?

***

This time I remembered to take the new road out along the Pine Mountain ridge. Even if it weren't all the way finished, I figured it had to be better than driving back over that logging road from Stoney Fork into Harlan like I done the last time, so I got in the car and drove south towards Middlesboro before turning due east at Wasioto.

I had plenty of gas in the tank to get me there and back and was making good time—that is, 'til I hit a patch of unfinished roadbed at the Milus crossroads and lost control of the car in the loose dirt and gravel. When I hit the brakes, the rear end went into a slide and spun bass-ack'ards off the side of the road.

I figured I was in for a rough ride all the way down to the treeline, but the car's back bumper plowed into a mound of dirt and gravel that slowed me down enough so that I didn't go flying off the side of the mountain.

But the rear tires slid into a runoff ditch and I was stuck up to the axle.

It took a minute for my head to stop spinning and my heart to stop pounding while the dust settled.

The hard stop killed the engine, so I set the hand brake and pushed on my door to climb out. But it was stuck shut and wouldn't open, so I held onto the steering wheel and crawled across the seat to let myself out on the other side.

I could stand up in the ditch after I got out but had a hard time finding my footing in the loose dirt and kept sliding back down every time I got up past the front bumper. Finally I give up and leaned back on the fender to catch my breath, which was when I heard a voice drift down from above.

"Up here, young feller."

I was able to make out the dim outline of a old man in overalls. He stood at the crest of the drop-off made by the bulldozers when they cut through the mountain.

"You alright down there?" he hollered.

I waved and nodded to let him know I heard him, then watched as he disappeared from view.

I was starting to wonder if he was coming back when he showed up again leading a team of mules across the edge of the embankment. They was dragging a pair of logging chains behind, I noticed, kicking up dust as they plodded along.

"Got away from ya, did she?" the old man called down after stopping the mules.

"Lost her in the gravels," I hollered up.

"You ain't the first," he told me. "Looks like you could use a little he'p."

I turned and looked back at the car like I was just then figuring that out.

"I'm in a fix alright," I agreed, turning back around.

"Well, I reckon Jenny and her sister here can pull you outta there."

"I'd appreciate it," I told him.

I watched as he turned the mules to pay out one of the logging chains down the embankment to me.

"If'n you can hook that snakin' chain to yer vehicle," he called down, "we'll haul you out."

I nodded and took hold of the heavy chain, dragged it underneath the bumper, and wrapped it around the front axle. When I climbed out, I give him a wave and he give his mules the signal to commence to pulling.

The Model A lurched forward, but the rear wheels was dragging behind, plowing through the dirt and gravel instead of rolling.

"Hold up!" I hollered.

The chain went slack and I clambered around the side of the car, crawled back in the passenger door, and let off the parking brake.

"Okay!" I yelled, motioning for the mules to start pulling again.

The car's chassis groaned, then settled down to the chain and rolled up the hillside with me still in it.

At the top, the old man stopped the team while I hopped out to crawl back underneath and unhook the chain. The mules stood stock still, waiting for a signal.

I climbed out from under the car, filthy from crawling in the dirt, and started brushing myself off.

That's when the old man first noticed my badge.

"Chasin' somebody?" he asked, narrowing his eyes at it.

"No sir, just on my way to Harlan to see a man about a dog," I answered, laughing to myself. "Mighty glad you happened by, though."

"Just come back from hauling logs down to the mill," he told me. "Road company cuts 'em down and pays me to haul 'em."

"Lucky for me," I said, reaching for my wallet.

"You can put that away," he told me.

"You ought to let me pay you something," I argued.

"No need for it. Jenny and her sister don't mind pulling a car out of a ditch ever' now and again. After all, they's a sight easier'n logs," he grinned. "Logs ain't got wheels!"

I laughed and said, "Well sir, I'm sure grateful to ya—and to Jenny and her sister, too."

As he led the team away, I got back in the car, worried that it might not start up again. But after a couple of cranks, she come back to life, blowing a cloud of white smoke out the back as I adjusted the throttle.

***

Even after running off the road, I made it to Harlan a good half hour before dark and parked out front of the courthouse the way I done before.

The clock over the courthouse door said it was a little after five, and no sooner had I shut down the engine than Lester Ball pulled up beside me.

"Where you been?" he asked after rolling down his window.

"I got hung up," I told him, which weren't a lie.

"Well, get in," he said, shaking his head.

"When you gonna tell me what's this about?" I asked as I crawled in beside him.

"You'll find out when we get there," he told me as he backed the car out into the street.

We drove around the block and parked in the alley back of the *Corner Cafe*, beside Jack's flatbed truck. I recognized it right off, even though the dog weren't setting on the back like usual.

We got out and went to the back door. Lester knocked and I heard a bolt slide on the inside.

"'Bout time," Big Sal complained when she opened the door to us. "The boy's in the kitchen."

We followed close on her heels as Sally walked across the empty dining room and pushed through the swinging door. I noticed a handmade CLOSED sign out in the front window as we passed, and inside was Jack Grimes setting in a ladderback chair by the icebox, stripping pieces of meat off a chicken bone and leaning over to feed them to the hound setting at his feet.

"Who said you could feed that dog in here," Sally scolded him right off.

"You said I was to wait," Jack answered without looking up nor speaking to me or the jailer neither one, "and Blue was getting hungry."

"I said you could feed him out back," Sally complained. "And where's the cat?" she asked, looking around the kitchen.

"Hiding under the stove," Jack answered with a half grin.

Sally give him a hard look, then stepped over to the sink for a bowl. We all watched as she went to the icebox, poured out cream from a pitcher, and set the bowl by the stove, turning her head towards the dog to say, "This ain't for you," as she stooped down to coax the cat out.

The jailer and me hadn't said a word while this was going on, but then I asked Jack, "Why are you here?"

"Hiding out," he told me.

"Hiding out?" I frowned. "Who from?"

"Not you, if that's what you're asking."

"Then who?" I said.

The boy looked from me to Lester. "Ain't you told him?"

"Told me what?" I asked both of them.

"It's about your brother," Jack answered.

"My brother?" I asked him, stunned.

"You're looking for him, ain't ya?"

I turned to Lester. "What've you told him?"

"I ain't told him nothing," Lester shrugged. "He's the one told *me*."

"How do you even know my brother?" I asked Jack.

"*Me*-Curt," he said, answering my question in one word. "You ain't the only one of your fam'ly ever come to Pickerin Holler, you know—only for different reasons."

"You mean Billy was with that bootlegger Henry Yeager," I said, putting two and two together.

Sally, done with feeding the cat, stood up and put her hands on her hips.

"If you girls are done catching up on all your kinfolk," she said, scowling mostly at Lester, "then maybe you can get this done and over with before somebody gets wind he's here?"

"Get *what* done and over with?" I asked, looking from one to the other of them. "What's this all about?"

"Sal's hiding your boy here from the gun thugs," Lester told me.

"Gun thugs? Why?"

"You tell him," Lester said, turning to Jack. "It was your idea to call him."

"Now just a dang minute," I said. "I ain't about to get involved in something that ain't even in my jurisdiction."

"Maybe not," Jack answered, "but if you want to know where your brother is, then you got to swear you'll get me out of this town."

"You got a truck," I said. "Git your own self out."

"How far you think I'd get before they run me down?" he asked.

"Run you down for what?" I asked, but Big Sal butt in before he could answer.

"Lester," she said, "less'n you're gonna make yourself useful and mop these floors for me, it's past time you and these other two got gone. I'm the one taking a chance here, you know."

I started to get a sinking feeling I ought t've stayed in Pineville.

"We got to go," Lester said.

"You got that right," Big Sal told him.

"Go where?" I asked.

"Out to my brother Boyd's place in Evarts."

"Why?"

"I'll explain on the way."

Jack clicked his tongue for his hound and we all followed Big Sal out to the back door. She opened it for us, then peered out into the darkening alley.

"All clear," she said.

"Be sure and lock up," the jailer told her on our way out.

***

The hound was already up on back of the flatbed by the time the rest of us got outside.

"We'll take the car," Lester told me.

Then to Jack, he said, "Stay close—and keep the lights switched off."

We pulled out of the alley, made a right turn back to the square and then a left that took us behind the court-house, out of town.

"What about my car?" I asked as the jailer switched on his lights so we could see the road.

"You can get it later," he told me. "Won't nobody bother it under the street lights."

"I need to call my deputy," I told him.

"You can do that when we get to Evarts," he said. "Boyd's got a telephone at the house."

"How far is it?" I asked.

"Not more'n a half hour," he answered, and in another minute we was out of town, heading east on a county road with Jack Grimes and his hound close behind, following our lights.

"Okay," I said, "it's time to tell me what's going on here and why you're taking me to your brother's place."

"You said you wanted to find your brother, didn't you?"

"How's this helping me find him?" I asked.

"The boy knows where he's at, but we can't go riding into a coal camp without getting stopped by the 'socia-tion's protection police, not without Boyd anyhow."

"So your brother's going with us? I thought he'd give up on being sheriff."

"Not when it comes to Devil Jim," he answered.

"Who?" I asked.

"Jim Jenkins—one of Boyd's deputies. The miners call him 'Devil Jim' on account of how rough he is on 'em."

"What's he got to do with this?"

"He's the one pistol-whipped the miner up at Lynch, the mining camp I told you about before."

"So Boyd don't like his deputies beating up miners. What's that got to do with my brother?"

"The boy said it was two agin one, and when he seen 'em knock the teeth out of the man's head with the butt of a gun, he stepped in to try and put a stop to it."

"So your brother's after the boy—after Jack—for fighting with his deputy?" I asked.

"No," Lester answered, "he's after Devil Jim and your brother for beating up that miner and the boy both. Why didn't you tell me it was your brother you was looking fer in the first place?"

"That's my business," I told him.

"It is until it ain't," he answered.

"What's that s'posed to mean?" I asked.

"Far as Boyd's concerned, it means your brother's on the wrong side of the law. It was him helped Devil Jim beat up that miner."

I felt sick to my stomach—like I'd swallered raw eggs.

***

With Jack and his dog close on our tail, we drove another ten minutes in dark silence 'til we turned off on a old wagon road that led up to a two-story farmhouse and barn nestled in a cove between two black hills.

We was met at the house by a pack of yelping curs that appeared from nowhere, and that brung a pie-faced bald man out on the porch. All he was wearing was red flannel underwear and a pair of plain black pull-on boots like mine.

"That's Boyd," Lester told me as he brung the sheriff's car to a squealing stop in the yard.

Jack pulled his truck up on my side and stopped.

"Who's that with you?" the sheriff called out to his brother as Lester opened his door to get out.

"It's the Bell County sheriff, Boyd," Lester hollered back as the dogs swarmed his legs. "If you'll put some pants on, maybe he'll come up and shake your hand."

He walked towards the house as I got out and was welcomed by the dogs, all wagging their tails and jumping around me as I made my way around the front of the car.

"I was in the john when you drove up, if it's any of your damn business," Lester's brother told him, then he turned to go back in the house.

"Don't mind Boyd," Lester told me. "Like this bunch, his bark's worse'n his bite. He's been holed up here since the election, and it ain't helped his disposition none."

We looked back to see if Jack was following us to the house, but he was busy with the hound—tying him up to keep him away from that bunch on the ground, I figured —so we headed for the front door without him.

By the time we got inside, Boyd was coming down from upstairs, buttoning a pair of pants as he went. His galluses hung from the waist.

"What happened to I.D.?" the sheriff asked me when he stopped at the bottom of the steps to pull the suspenders up on his shoulders.

"Retired," I answered, figuring a simple answer was best.

"Since when did they start letting tadpoles like you run for sheriff in Bell County?" he asked.

I could feel my face and ears getting hot.

"I was I.D.'s deputy for two year," I said, trying not to let it rile me, then turned to Lester. "I need to use the tele-phone."

Boyd kept on. "Mighty young to be a sheriff, though."

"On the wall in the kitchen," Lester told me, grinning as he pointed me down the hallway to the back of the house.

"Must not've cared much for you," Boyd trailed after me, "if he let you run for sheriff."

"He tried telling me," I answered, forcing a smile, "but I guess I weren't listening."

And that's when we heard the dogs yapping out in the yard again.

Boyd looked alarmed.

Lester said, "The boy and his hound's still out there," and Boyd went to a closet under the stairs and took out a rifle for his brother and a shotgun for hisself.

"Where's your sidearm?" the sheriff asked me.

"Back at my car," I told him.

He shook his head in disbelief and turned away to go close the still-open front door.

Lester took off up the stairs.

I followed Boyd to a window at the side of the house nearest the road.

Peering out at the truck, I could see that the hound was gone from the back, but I couldn't see Jack nowhere.

"Who's out there?" I asked Boyd over the nervous barking of the farm dogs outside.

"Cain't tell yet," he answered as he stared out the win-dow.

A set of headlights was coming our way, but that's all we could make out 'til the car pulled up and stopped short of the house.

"What the hell," Boyd said when the driver's door opened and a towering dark figure stepped out into the night.

"Lester?" he hollered up the stairs.

"It's Jim, alright," his brother called down, "and he's got somebody with him."

"Who is it?" Boyd asked, but whatever else him and his brother might've had in mind to say or do got lost in the blast of a shotgun out near the flatbed truck. It busted one of the car's headlights, sending up a cloud of smoke and scattering the dogs.

The man behind the car door drawed a pistol, ducked down, and took a potshot towards the barn before scrambling back inside.

The car backed away from the house in a fit of dust and gravel, then turned tail and run.

"That back-biting son of a bitch," Boyd growled as the car sped away down the farm road and Lester come running down the stairs.

He was out of breath.

"I think the boy's been hit!" he said. "I seen him go down."

When we got outside, Jack was standing at the back of the truck, leaning over on the bed. The shotgun was laying in front of him. The hound stood at his feet.

The other dogs, now gone quiet, gathered around us like gawkers in a schoolyard fistfight.

Lester looked the boy up and down in the dim light, pulling at his shirt as he moved around him.

"Where you hit?" he asked.

Jack shook his head, saying, "I don't know."

"Here it is," Lester said, pointing to a dark stain growing on the boy's left side, right at the shoulder.

"Get him in the house," Boyd said.

Lester put a arm 'round his waist and I got on the other side to help.

"I'm alright," Jack protested, but even in the dark, I could see he was pale as watered-down milk.

I didn't notice the dog was following us until we got in the kitchen and set Jack down in a chair. The hound sidled up and laid his head on the boy's leg.

Boyd got a towel from the sink, pumped water onto it, and brought it to Lester. Jack winced as the jailer tore a bigger hole in the shirt to get at the wound.

"I seen worse," he declared, then give Jack the towel and told him to keep it pressed there to stop the bleeding.

"We better get him to the hospital," Boyd said. "He'll need a doctor to dig out the slug."

"I ain't going to no hospital," Jack swore.

"You ain't got no choice," Boyd told him, then motioned for me and Lester to get him to his feet.

It must've hurt, but he never complained one time while we carried him out to the car between the two of us, but by the time we got him there, his chin had fell to his chest and his head was lolling back and forth with every step.

Boyd got in and started the engine while Lester and me laid the boy out in the back. There weren't room for all four of us, so I went to the truck while Lester climbed in beside his brother. When I rounded the back of the bed to pick up Jack's shotgun, I found the dog waiting on me.

"Alright," I told the hound, "but I'm driving."

***

The city hospital was located off to one side of the square, opposite the side of the Harlan County courthouse where I'd left my car. It didn't take us long to get there the way Boyd drove, meaning like a bat out of hell, with me and the dog bouncing around in the truck, trying to keep up.

After we pulled up to the front entrance, I jumped out to help get the boy out of the car. The hound got nervous, so I let him follow me.

Me and Lester carried Jack into the hospital with Boyd leading the way. By then he was barely able to put one foot in front of the other, so we had to drag him along between us like a drunk. At the door, I told the hound to "stay" and he did.

Inside, Boyd started giving orders to the nurses, and when two orderlies showed up to take the boy off our hands, he told me and Lester to go back out and keep a eye out for Devil Jim.

"In case he shows up here," he told us.

"I wouldn't put it past him," Lester said as we turned to leave.

"Ain't we kinda setting ducks here?" I asked him on the way out.

He agreed with me.

"Maybe we ought to ditch the truck, then," he said.

"Where?"

"I got a idea, but they's something else I want to do before that."

"And what's that?"

"I'll tell you when we get there."

"Well, take me by my car first, will ya?" I asked him.

"What for?"

"I'll tell ya when we get there," I said, throwing his own words back at him.

The dog, standing and waiting by the door all that time, followed us out to the truck, and when he seen us climb in the cab, he hopped up on the flatbed.

Lester cranked the engine and backed out into the street, and a minute later we was parked beside my car at the front of the courthouse.

Soon as Lester brung the truck to a squealing stop, I jumped out and went to the back of my car. I opened the trunk, took out my gunbelt, and strapped it on as I walked back towards Lester.

"Little late for that, ain't it?" he said as I got back in.

I shrugged, then asked him where we was headed.

"To check on Big Sal," he told me.

"Why?"

"How do you think Jim knowed where to look for the boy?"

"You think Sal told him?" I asked.

"Not of her own free will if she did," he answered.

***

When we passed in front of the *Corner Cafe*, I noticed the closed sign still up in the window, and the lights was out.

"I don't think she's here," I said.

"Maybe," Lester answered, "but I'd feel better if we checked."

We drove around the corner and into the dark alley behind the place, parking at the back door again.

Lester left the truck running and got out. I watched as he took hold of the door knob and turned it.

"It's open," he said, motioning me to follow him in.

Just inside the door, he stopped to listen, then called out.

"Sal?"

Getting no answer, he called again and moved towards the swinging door leading into the kitchen. A narrow ribbon of dim light shown between the door and the casing, and as Lester pushed the door open, a dark shape flew out across his toes.

I drew in my breath and grabbed for my service pistol but broke into a grin when I seen what it was.

"Damned cat!" he swore before pushing on through to the kitchen.

I followed close on his heels as he went through, but the grin disappeared when we found Big Sal in a chair by the sink, holding a towel to her face.

"What happened?" Lester asked her as we stepped closer. "Why didn't you answer?"

She shook her head without taking the towel away.

"Let me see," Lester said as he pulled her arm down, revealing a nasty split in her lip.

"Who done this?" he asked her.

"Who do you think?" she winced.

"Devil Jim?"

She nodded, bringing the towel back up to her swollen mouth.

She was mad, I could tell, but hurt, too.

I stepped to the faucet and poured her a glass of water.

"Here," I said, offering it to her.

She took a sup, half of it dribbling down her chin, then handed it back to me, shaking her head and dabbing at her lip with the towel again.

Lester knelt down to get a closer look at her face.

"Them sons-a-bitches," he said, raising her chin.

Big Sal winced again. Her left eye was bloodshot and she was already getting a shiner.

Lester took the towel from her and handed it to me.

"Wet this," he said, and I stepped quick to do it.

"I didn't tell," I heard Sal mumble through her swole-up lip.

"It don't matter," Lester told her. "He already knowed where to start looking anyways."

I give the towel back and he dabbed at her face, gentle as he would a child's.

"They was two," she said, holding up two fingers, and I felt sick to my stomach again.

"Can you get up?" he asked her.

She nodded.

"Alright, then," he said, "we're taking you home."

We helped her to her feet and started walking her towards the door.

"Wait," she said. "My coat."

I grabbed it off the nail by the door and helped her on with it while Lester held her arm. When we got to the back door, I walked her out and around the back of the truck while Lester shut the cafe door and climbed in to drive. I helped her up onto the seat and got in beside her.

On the way out of the alley, Lester told Sal what happened out at the farm, including the part about the boy being shot and us taking him to the hospital.

"He's alright, though, ain't he?" she asked in spite of the pain.

"You don't worry about the boy," Lester told her. "Ain't none of this your fault."

It was the last we talked about it before getting her to her house, which was close by as it turned out. Not two blocks off the square, Lester pulled into her gravel and slag driveway, getting close as he could to her front door.

"We'll walk you in," he said.

"I can walk myself in," she told us.

"Like hell you will," Lester answered as he climbed out.

"I ain't afraid of that big ape," she spat in spite of her split lip.

You're braver'n you ought to be then, I thought as I got out and offered her a hand down.

She slid across the seat and I eased her out down to the ground.

"You got the key?" Lester asked her from the porch.

"It ain't locked," she told him.

He looked at her, shook his head, and started to say something but changed his mind.

He opened the door and I helped her inside.

We waited while she switched on a light in the hall.

"You go check the kitchen," Lester told me. "I'll look around the rest of the place."

Sally started trying to get out of her coat. I stopped to help her, but as I turned back around, I spotted a shadow moving up the porch steps. Sally must've sensed it too. She turned to look, leaving me holding her coat.

Jack's hound had invited hisself to dinner.

"Well," she said, her hands on her hips, "come on in."

"I'll get him," I told her as I handed her the coat.

"No," she said, touching my arm as the dog padded down the hall towards us, "leave him be."

"You sure?"

"Can't think of nobody better to guard the place, can you?"

"S'pose not," I told her, "but most likely he's just hungry."

"Me too," she said and started down the hall behind him, still wearing her coat.

I followed.

"Hey, Sal," I called after her.

She turned.

"You got a telephone I can use?"

***

Turned out I was too late calling the switchboard at the courthouse, so I give some thought to calling Floyd at home to let him know I was stuck in Harlan but decided not to bother him.

After checking the kitchen and locking Sal's doors, me and Lester left to go back to the hospital. On the way, he decided it might be a good time to swap out the boy's truck for my car at the courthouse.

"It won't hurt to keep Jim guessing where we are," Lester said about Boyd's deputy and I agreed.

We drove to the square, now lit up by street lamps, and parked the truck next to the Model A. I'd left the key in the ignition and switched it on, then re-set the choke and stepped on the starter, but nothing happened. I tried again, this time checking the spark lever and fuel switch first to be sure they was set proper. After I tried it a third time with no luck, I called for Lester to climb out of the truck and raise the hood to look in at the engine while I tried one more time.

When nothing happened again, he said, "Maybe it's the batt'ry."

"I ain't had no trouble with it," I told him through the windshield, but not mentioning I'd run off the road at Milus on the way in.

"Well, leave it," he told me, dropping the hood back in place. "We ain't got time to fool with it right now."

I crawled out, taking the key with me this time, and climbed back into the cab of the truck with Lester.

"Bad luck," he said as he started it back up.

***

At the hospital, we pulled in beside the sheriff's car again. Lester let the truck idle as we set there under the street lamp.

"Are we waitin' on Boyd?" I asked.

"I ain't sure," he answered, so I recommended we go inside.

"To get warm, if nothing else," I told him.

In the lobby, Lester walked up to the nurse at the front desk.

"We brung a boy with a gunshot in here a little while ago," he said.

"Second floor," she told us.

"He gonna be alright?" Lester asked her.

"You'll have to ask the nurse," she said.

"You got a phone I can use?" I asked, rethinking that call to Floyd after the way the Model A was acting.

She pointed to one on a table next to a chair on the other side of the room.

"I'll be up in a minute," I told Lester and put in that call to Floyd, which took a load off my mind, then headed up to the second floor and found the room with the help of the floor nurse, but when I got there, I was surprised to find Jack awake and setting up in the bed.

Boyd was setting in a chair in the corner, reading a newspaper.

"Where's Lester?" I asked him.

"Toilet," he answered.

"Hurt much?" I asked Jack, pointing to the gauze bandage around his shoulder.

"Naw," he told me. "Where's Blue?"

"We left him with Big Sal," I told him. "Said she'd make sure he got fed."

He laid his head back on the pillow and closed his eyes.

"Well," Boyd said, standing up, "we might as well go."

"What about Lester?" I asked.

"He'll catch up."

I took a last look at Jack asleep in his hospital bed, then followed Boyd out of the room and back down to the lobby, where we found Lester waiting on us. The three of us went back outside, stopping in front of the boy's truck for a smoke. Boyd took a pack of cigarettes out of his breast pocket and offered me one. Lester took out one of his own and we all lit up, which was when I decided then was as good a time as any to confess that I'd been looking for my brother Billy this whole time.

I took a deep draw off my smoke, let it out, and begun the sorry tale about Billy and how he'd come to be in Harlan. I told about his bootlegging and gun-running in Bell County with the Baldwin-Felts "bull" Henry Yeager—the one who shot I.D.—and about his running off to Newport only to get hisself shot and then on to Cleveland where he got mixed up with a even bigger gang of criminals.

At the end of it, I even told how I come to find out from Bureau Agent Schilder in Cincinnati that Billy was supposed to be in Harlan now, working as a Baldwin-Felts "bull" hisself.

"I just didn't want to say nothing about it before," I told them, trying to explain myself, "at least not 'til I found out if he was really here or not."

After that, Boyd took a draw off his cigarette and throwed it to the ground.

"Well, Lester," he said to his brother, "looks like you're damn lucky you ain't been found dangling from the end of a rope out in the county som'ers."

I looked from one to the other, confused.

"And you might be yet," he told him, "if the 'sociation gets wind of it."

"What's going on here?" I asked. "Did I miss something?"

They looked at each other but didn't answer.

"What is it?" I asked again.

"Lester's took it on hisself to go to work for the goldang gover'ment, that's what!" Boyd said like he was spitting the words out on the ground.

I looked at Lester, my head cocked to one side.

"What's he talking about?" I asked.

Lester blinked, then bit his lower lip.

"I'm the one told the Bureau your brother was here," he suddenly confessed.

I didn't know what to think.

"Not just him," he went on, reading my face, "ever' damn one of them 'protection police' the 'sociation's been hiring and bringing in here week after week."

I frowned and shook my head.

"But if you already knowed my brother was here . . .," I started to say.

"I didn't," Lester interrupted me, "not 'til you told me. All I been doing is reporting on the men being picked up at the railway station by them other Baldwin-Felts sons-a-bitches the 'sociation's already set down on us. They pick 'em up here at the station and take 'em out to the mining camps. I don't know their names, I just report how many of 'em they are and a description—what they look like."

I was still shaking my head, trying to take it all in, when Boyd butt in.

"They're building up a private army in here is what they're doing. And what do you think the gover'ment's gonna do about it? Same damn thing happened in Logan County and all the fed'ral gover'ment done there was send in soldiers to help put down the miners, that's what."

Lester turned on him then.

"Well, I ain't just gonna give up and watch it happen like you're a'doin'!" he told his brother, "and if you'd seen what them bastards done to Sal tonight, you might change your mind!"

Boyd scowled. "What? What'd they do to Sal?"

"Devil Jim set down on her at the diner, that's what," Lester told him, flicking away his cigarette. "He went looking for the boy and took it out on Sal."

"Where's she now?" Boyd asked.

Lester nodded in my direction. "We took her home."

"She bad hurt?" he asked.

"Wix done worse'n that when he was still around," Lester told him.

Boyd studied the ground for a second, then looked up at me.

"You need to go," he said, "tonight—and take the boy with you."

"What?" I asked. "Why?"

"This ain't your fight, and him being here is making things worse."

"Boyd's right," Lester told me. "They ain't nothing more you can do here, and taking the boy out of the county might settle this thing with Jim and the 'socia-tion."

"Ain't they still gonna be looking for him?" I asked.

"More'n likely," Lester admitted.

I dropped the butt of my cigarette to the sidewalk and looked down, thinking while I snubbed it out with the toe of my boot.

"What about my brother?" I asked when I looked back up.

"He's made his bed," Boyd answered.

***

Next thing I knowed, Lester was driving me back to the courthouse to get my car, but I worried it might not start again. He stayed in the truck and kept it running while I opened the door and stepped in, leaving one leg out on the street. After checking the spark lever, I turned the key and stepped on the starter button, but nothing happened. I tried again, and then once more as Lester shut off the truck's engine and got out to help.

"I'll get the hand crank," he said, stepping back to the Model A's trunk.

After he'd threaded the crank in behind the front bumper, I set the spark and give him a thumbs up. Nothing happened on the first try, but she caught on the second crank and clattered to life, spewing white smoke out the tailpipe into the night air. The engine rocked 'til I got the choke adjusted, then settled down into a smooth idle.

Thank the Lord, I thought.

"Alright!" Lester said, then pulled the crank handle out, carried it back to the trunk for me, and shut the lid.

He climbed back in the truck and I followed him back to the hospital, waiting outside under the lights with the engine running while he went in to get the boy. In a minute or two, he come back out pushing a wheelchair down the walkway with Jack in it and Boyd right behind them.

They'd wrapped Jack's head and shoulders in a blanket to keep him warm and brung him around to the passenger side to put him in.

"Any trouble getting him out of there?" I asked, wondering if they'd had to ask permission and hoping it weren't from a doc like our'n if they did.

"I'm still sheriff here," Boyd reminded me, looking in as they hefted the boy from the chair to the seat.

Jack set stock still while I put the car in gear, backed out into the street, give Lester and Boyd a quick two-fingered wave, and pulled away.

When I looked back through the car's mirror, Lester was already back in the truck and Boyd was rolling the wheelchair back towards the hospital door.

It was a strange parting, and I wondered if I'd ever see either one of them again.

***

"Where's Blue?" was Jack's first words when got started out of town.

I'd near forgot about the dog.

I started to say we'd have to leave him, but considering what all the boy had been through, I said, "I reckon we can go by and get him—that is, if I can find the place again."

"The diner?" he asked.

"No," I told him, "he's at Sally's house here in town, but I got to find it again."

I made a hard left at the first street we come to and turned around, heading back the way Lester took us to Sally's.

I looked for anything familiar and finally recognized a two-story brick house on one corner. I remembered it on account of its drive-through portico and thinking it must belong to some rich banker there in town.

We turned there and found Sally's house on the next corner, one block over.

"This is it," I told Jack as I pulled off the street into her gravel driveway. "Stay put."

I left the car running and went up on her porch to knock. When I did, I seen the hall light come on through a pane of frosted glass in the door. Big Sal opened it a crack, then wider when she recognized who it was. I noticed a dark bruise coming up on her jaw now and another under her swole-up eye. She had on a housecoat and was slipping something with a muzzle into the side pocket.

"You carrying a gun now?" I asked.

"It was my husband's. I figure it might come in handy if Jim Jenkins shows up here."

"Well, I come for the boy's dog," I told her.

"That him out yonder?" she asked, pointing a finger towards the car.

"Yep," I answered.

"He alright?"

"He will be."

"Where you takin' him?"

"Back to Pineville," I told her, "with me."

She hesitated, studying my face, then said, "I'll get the dog."

She turned and walked back through the hall towards the kitchen. I waited out on the porch.

The hound, plodding along behind her as she come back, stopped beside her at the door.

"Thanks, Sal," I said, then, "Let's go," to the dog, but it didn't follow when I turned to leave.

"Well, go on," Big Sal told him, "I didn't take you to raise," but still the hound didn't budge.

She reached down to push him out by his rump and I'd started back to grab him by the scuff of the neck when a familiar sound brung him out running. He cleared the steps in one leap and bounded to the car.

Jack had rolled down his window and clicked his tongue, and that's all it took.

I turned back to Big Sal.

"You gonna be alright here on your own?" I asked her.

"You ain't got to worry about me," she said, patting the pocket she'd slipped the gun into before. "Now go on, it's cold out here."

I said good night and walked away as she shut the door behind me and throwed the lock.

At the car, I opened the door and let the animal in the back seat. He leapt up, set down, and laid his long snout over the front onto Jack's shoulder. Jack smiled and lifted his good arm to pat the top of his dog's head.

***

In spite of the trouble I'd had out on the new road, I decided to go back through the crossroads at Milus again, then on to Wasioto and down the mountain to Pineville. Course that meant taking the boy home with me for the evening, less'n I decided to put him in jail for the night. In the end, I decided it'd be easier to take him home with me, and, besides, Ma always liked the boy.

Because of the late hour, I parked in the alley and slipped him in through the back of the house to keep from disturbing Ma. I helped him to the living room, and let him sleep on the couch. I tiptoed upstairs in my stocking feet to go to bed for the night. Problem with that plan was I overslept the next morning and got woke up by Ma tapping like a woodpecker on my bedroom door. I opened my eyes and stared at the ceiling.

"Sam," she was saying.

"I'm up, Ma," I told her, jumping out of bed to pull on my britches.

When I opened the door, she was still standing there, waiting.

"*Why* is Eugene sleeping downstairs on the sofa?" she asked.

"I didn't want to disturb you," I said.

She give me a hard look. "That ain't what I mean."

"We had some trouble in Harlan," I told her then, "and I brung him here to stay 'til I can work something out."

"What kind of trouble? And why is his shoulder all bandaged up?

"Is he still asleep?" I asked, side-stepping her questions.

"He is, but it's a wonder. It's freezing down there and he's only got the one blanket. You could've at least got the one off your brother's bed for him if you weren't going to bring him up here. And what happened to him? Is he bad hurt?"

"Well, no," I told her. "I mean, he did get shot, but—"

"Shot! Is he going to be alright?"

"He'll mend. They got the bullet out at the hospital in Harlan. I'll get the blanket off Tick's bed for him," I said, edging my way around to escape to his room.

"It's a little late for that," she told me. "Besides, I already done it."

I guess she was finished scolding me because she let me by to go to the toilet.

"Let me know when you two are ready for something to eat," she told me as she headed back downstairs and I headed to the bathroom in the hall.

When I got done, I went down and checked on Jack.

"Jack," I whispered from the door, but he didn't budge. He was laying on his right side facing the back of the couch, the same way I left him the night before.

I stepped closer and whispered again.

"Jack."

"*Mmmf*," he moaned, the sound muffled by the extry blanket Ma laid over him.

Best to leave sleeping dogs lay, I thought, and that's when I remembered the hound!

I stepped into my boots where I'd left them at the bottom of the stairs and hurried out to the car. When I opened the back door, there he was, laid out across the seat cushion wide awake with his head on his paws, patient as a owl.

When I let him out, he run up to the back porch with his nose to the ground—tracking Jack's scent from the night before, I figured. When he got to the door, he stopped and waited for me.

"Stay," I told him and he did.

Inside, I found Jack setting at the kitchen table with the hospital blanket wrapped 'round him like a Indian. He was bleary-eyed as a drunk with a three-day hangover.

"I'm fixin' eggs," Ma told me from the stove. "You ready to eat?"

"All I want is coffee right now," I told her, "but I think the dog could eat something."

"The dog?" she asked, turning from the stove to look around like she thought maybe I'd let it in the kitchen.

"He's out on the porch," I told her. "You got any scraps I can give him?"

"Look in the icebox," she said, going back to the eggs. "There might be some leftovers in there."

"Alright," I said, opening it to rummage around.

I found a plate of greasy beans and meatloaf and carried it to the table.

"What about you, Eugene?" Ma asked. "You hungry yet?"

"No, ma'am," he answered, looking at the plate in my hand. I could swear he turned green.

"Not this," I told him. "It's for the dog."

"I'll take it to him," he said, getting up in spite of his shoulder.

I handed it over, and while he was out on the porch with the hound I grabbed a cup from off the cupboard to pour myself some hot coffee from the pot on the stove.

"I was just thinking," I said to Ma as I poured. "What would you say to letting the boy stay here a day or two?"

She stopped and turned to face me, her hands hovering over the skillet.

"This ain't gonna end up like the last time, is it?" she asked me, almost scowling.

I figured she was most likely talking about the time Dewey Grimes come to the house drunk, looking for his two girls and threatening to shoot up the place 'til Virgil got there and cold-cocked him up side the head with his service pistol.

"There ain't nobody looking for him," I said, "leastways nobody in Bell County."

"Well I should hope not," she told me. "I had about all the excitement I could stand with that pa of his this summer."

"There's no chance of that now, Ma," I reminded her. "He's gone for good."

"Well," she said, "Genia and them children are better off is all I can say."

I nodded and took a sup of coffee.

***

After breakfast, I left Jack at the house with Ma and headed over to the courthouse.

Floyd was there in the front office.

"Anything come up while I was gone?" I asked him after hanging my jacket on the hook behind my door.

He hesitated, which got my attention.

"What is it?" I asked from the doorway to my office.

"It's Alvey."

"What about him?"

"The chief wants to offer him the jailer's job."

"Since when?"

"Since Parnell Knuckels quit," he told me.

"Quit?" I asked. "What happened?"

"Come in yesterday and told Virgil he was leaving is all I know. Said he was going to work for his pa at the mill in Lone Jack."

"Huh," I answered, but the truth is, I weren't all that surprised. Parnell only had the job at the jail on account of

Virgil being old friends with his pa, and I figured his pa told him he might as well leave before he got let go now that Virgil was fixing to leave.

"So Alvey wants to know if it's alright with you if he takes the job," Floyd said, looking a little uneasy. "He don't want to stir nothing up 'tween you and Lovis Evans."

"You can tell him it's fine with me. And tell him I'll fight to keep him on after Lovis takes over too. Half that job belongs to the county, you know."

"I'll tell him, Sheriff," Floyd answered, "and thanks."

He looked relieved. Course, he couldn't know I was more worried about Lovis coming in and replacing every officer he had with some kin of his or some crony's kin than I was about Alvey taking the job. Trouble with Lovis, he was like a dog in the manger. If he got wind I wanted Alvey to be the jailer, he'd like as not fire him for spite.

I was still standing in the doorway when my telephone started ringing.

"Sam," Verda said when I picked up.

"Yes, Verda."

"I've got a call for you from the Harlan County Sheriff's Office."

Lord, what now? I thought. "They say who it is?"

"No."

I let out a heavy sigh. "Okay, put 'em on."

I recognized the voice right off. It was Lester Ball.

"I know you was just here," he told me without even saying hello, "but you ain't gonna believe who come in here looking for Boyd this morning."

"Hold on a second," I told him, then said "Verda" into the phone stern as I could without scolding and waited for the click.

"Alright, go ahead," I told Lester.

"Your brother come in here this morning," he said.

"My brother? Why?"

"On account of the 'sociation. Said he's being set up to take the blame for a killing."

"What killing?" I asked.

"I think you'd better talk to him about that."

"Put him on, then," I said.

"No," the jailer told me, "you'll need to come to the courthouse. I've got him locked away for his own protection."

"Oh, hell!" I said, forgetting Floyd was setting right outside the door. I didn't care for him overhearing, I just didn't want to have to explain what was going on with my brother if I didn't have to.

Anyway, I agreed to go back to Harlan and left Floyd in charge while I hightailed it back across Pine Mountain again. It was getting to be like a regular part of the job!

The jailer met me at the front of the courthouse as soon as I pulled up in front and parked.

"Where's he at?" I asked as soon as I got out, picking up where we'd left off.

He pointed the way, and I followed him down the hall.

"In here," he told me when we come to a oversized metal door at the end.

He fit his key into the lock and swung it open.

"Where's this go?" I asked.

"Into the basement," he answered. "It's the old jail."

"In the cellar? Why's he down there?"

"It's where I keep special prisoners sometimes."

"Special?"

"I've got the only key, and this is the only way in or out. You head on down and we'll be there in a minute."

"Where you going?" I asked. "And who's *we*?"

"Boyd and me," he answered. "He said to let him know when you got here."

"Where is he?"

"Waiting in his office."

"I thought he'd quit coming in."

"He's come in for *this*," Lester told me. "Go on ahead. We'll be down in a minute. Meantime, your brother can tell you why he's here."

The jailer started back up the hall, his key ring jangling as he walked.

I held the heavy door open, stuck my head in, and found myself gaping into a black hole with only one dim light overhead—like the mouth of a drif' mine cut into the side of a mountain. The damp, musty smell of a moldy cellar hit me square in the face.

I stepped inside, onto on a narrow landing at the top of a set of metal stairs that led down one side of the block wall. Holding onto a rusty handrail, I felt my way down a dozen or so steps to the concrete floor at the bottom, where I found a switch for a couple of naked bulbs that hung from the ceiling. When I flipped them on, I was standing in front of two metal cages. It reminded me of a dungeon in a book I read in high school, *The Count of Monte Cristo*.

"Tick!" I hollered.

Getting no answer, I tried again.

"Tick!"

"Over here," he called out in a watery voice that didn't sound like him a'tall.

I found him tucked away in the cell to my right, setting on a cot shoved back against the block wall. I squinted through the bars, studying his shadowy face in the grainy light of the naked bulb overhead, and for the first time in my life, I seen my brother looking scared—and I mean cornered animal scared.

I tried the door. It was locked, like Lester had said.

"Lester told me there's been a killing," I told him.

"Who's Lester?" he asked.

"The jailer."

"Oh," he answered.

"Why'd you tell him you're being set up?"

I was waiting on his answer when the sound of heavy footfalls on the metal steps above interrupted us, getting Tick's nervous attention. His eyes widened and I turned to look, expecting to see the jailer and his brother.

"That you, Lester?" I called up the stairs, my words echoing off the high block walls.

"Stay where you are," a booming voice threatened from out of the darkness above, causing my brother to scurry like a rat in his cell. If he'd had claws, he might've tried to dig his way under the courthouse wall.

"It's Devil Jim," Tick hissed. "Don't let him at me!"

By then I could make out the deputy coming down the steps, Boyd Ball in front of him.

"Get away from that door," Jim ordered, and I took a step back from Tick's cell.

"All the way back," he warned, bringing a pistol out from behind the sheriff's back to wave me over as far as I could go.

"He'll kill me sure," my brother squawked in a panic.

I had no weapon and no place to run. I searched the sheriff's face for a sign of hope but found none as he got to the bottom of the stairs with the gun at his back.

Devil Jim shoved him off the last step towards the second cell, the empty one next to my brother's.

"Open it!" he demanded and Boyd lifted a jingling key ring to the lock, making me wonder what had happened to Lester.

He put the key in the lock but left it hanging.

"I said open it!" the deputy ordered, shoving the muzzle of the pistol into Boyd's back again.

Boyd, his face hard with rage, pulled the cell door open. It made a grating sound that set my teeth on edge.

"Get in," Jim ordered, pushing him forward by the shoulder, but just as Boyd started to move, the metal door at the top of the stairs slammed shut and the light there went out. I blinked, trying to make out who it was as I seen Jim take aim up the steps. He fired off his pistol with a blinding flash and deafening roar that made me jump back and cover both ears with the palms of my hands, but almost at that same time, a second boom and flash come from above. It felled the deputy, sending him reeling backwards towards the sheriff. His bearlike carcass slumped to the floor, where he leaned back against the open cell door.

Boyd, fast on his feet for a man his age, snatched the pistol from Jim's loose grip and passed it to me.

"Watch him!" he said as he started up the staircase.

"Is he dead?" I heard Tick call to me from his cell.

Above us, the jail door opened from the outside, letting in more light. Lester stepped through onto the landing. He switched the stairway light back on, and now I could see Boyd bent down over a body, but it weren't 'til I heard

Lester cry out "Sal!" that I knowed who it was, and it weren't 'til later on—after we'd drug Devil Jim inside the cell next to my brother's and locked him up for safekeeping and after Lester had run up to call a ambulance for Big Sal and they'd come and got her—that I learned how Boyd's turncoat deputy got the drop on all of us that morning.

"He walked in before Lester showed up and wanted the keys to the cellar jail," Boyd told me, "and when I told him to go to hell, he pulled his pistol on me. When Lester walked in, he got the worst of it."

"That happened right after I opened the hall door for you and went back to Boyd's office," Lester said. "Jim took the keys off'n me, thumped me over the head, and left me laying on the floor, senseless."

In spite of being shot in the belly, Devil Jim weren't done for yet. He was showing signs of life by the time the two fellers with the ambulance showed up to get Big Sal, so the three of us—me, Lester and Boyd—dragged his useless hide into the cell, after which Boyd slammed the door shut and locked him in, and which is when my brother, watching all this from the other cell, hollered out, "Hey, what about me?"

I raised one eyebrow and looked at Boyd for a answer.

"Well?" Tick demanded. "What about it?"

"Tell you what, Sheriff," Boyd said, ignoring my brother, "I'll remand him to your custody, but only on condition that you haul his hind end out of Harlan County this very day and make sure he stays out for as long as I'm sheriff here." Then, turning to Tick, he said, "Is that understood?"

"I'll make sure of it," I answered for both of us and Boyd opened his cell. I reached in and grabbed my brother by the arm, dragging him out and near pushing him up the stairs before he opened his mouth and ruined his chance.

When we got to the spot where Big Sal had fell, I stopped and pointed it out.

"That was Sally Howard," I told him, "the woman you beat up at the diner."

I wanted him to know he owed her.

"Why are you here, anyway?" he asked me. "What business is this of your'n?"

I was fed up.

"I ain't arguing with you," I told him. "Either you go back to Pineville with me or I hand you back over to the sheriff."

He looked at me like I'd pissed on his shoes.

***

I didn't know what to expect when I got home with my brother that day, but what we found when we pulled into the alley behind the house was Jack's hound lazin' out on the back porch. It stood up and watched us but stayed put as we got out of the car. Then Ma come out wiping her hands on her apron. She was followed by Jack, who was wearing a arm sling I figured Ma fashioned for him. The three of them stood side by side, watching and waiting.

I'd imagined Ma with tears in her eyes, rushing out and running off the porch with her arms outstretched to welcome her boys home, but, instead, she hardly raised a eyebrow. She stood there rigid as a fence post, giving my brother and me a hard and wary look as we walked up.

"Where you been?" she asked when we got to the bottom step.

"Harlan," I answered. "I went to find—"

"I ain't asking *you*," she said, narrowing her eyes at my brother. I'd never seen her so put out with him before.

They stood there looking each other dead in the eye, but he wouldn't answer.

"Are we gonna stand out here all day?" I asked, trying to break the spell.

"No use you coming in unless you're planning on changing your ways," Ma told him, but still Tick said nothing.

"Well?" I said, trying to goad him into answering.

And that's when he curled his lips into a snarl, turned on his heels, and walked away towards the car.

"Billy," Ma called after him, but he never even turned around.

I followed him through the yard, catching up and grabbing his arm as he got to the alley.

"Where you think you're going?" I asked.

"Away," he answered. "Let go of me!"

"Nothing doing," I said, hardening my grip.

"Dammit, Sam," he warned, "let go!"

"You're upsettin' Ma," I told him, but when I looked back to make a point of it, her and Jack had both gone back inside the house. Even the dog had laid back down like he didn't much care.

I let go his arm.

"Alright, I've let go," I said, holding up the palms of both hands. "What the hell's wrong with you?"

"It's the boy," he told me, tossing his head in the direction of the house.

"The boy? I asked. "What about him?"

"If they find out he ain't dead, my life won't be worth a plug nickel."

"If *who* finds out?" I asked, confused.

"The men who hired me."

"Why in hell would Baldwin-Felts care if the boy's alive or dead?"

Tick glared.

"You dumb ass," he said, "it ain't the agency who's out to get him, it's the association."

"The mine owners? Why would they care? Ain't it enough the boy's gone from there?"

He throwed it back at me.

"Don't you know what you've done? When they find out he left town with you, they'll figure I was in on it."

"In on what?"

"In on getting him out of Harlan and hiding him out here at the house, that's what."

I started to ask how they'd know, then remembered Devil Jim was still breathing when we left.

"What's so important to 'em about one boy who was only trying to keep a miner from getting his head stove in?" I asked.

He laughed in my face.

"You think they care one way or t'other about that? The boy's been working for the union. They're planning a strike to shut down the Lynch mine. Don't you know that? Why else would he be hiding out in that woman's diner?"

"Big Sal's place?" I asked.

"She was in on it," he told me, "using her place for meetings and such and hiding unionizers from the 'sociation. It's a wonder she weren't shot and killed before this. And she would've been too, I can tell you, if not for that interferin' sheriff and jailer."

I was still trying to get my head around all that when Tick turned away and started down the alley towards town.

"Where you goin'?" I called after him.

"I need a drink," he said over his shoulder and kept on walking.

That evening at supper, I asked Jack what he knowed about the union trying to shut down the mine at Lynch and found out he'd got a job there after he left Bell County.

"They's a war a'comin'," he told me, "and men will die."

**

My brother did come back to the house that night—or early the next morning, really, just before daybreak. Old man Lasley's hounds woke me up howling, and I got up to see what the ruckus was about.

I headed out of my room and into the upstairs hall— pulling my trousers on as I went—and run into Ma in her nightgown.

"What is it, Sam?"

By then the hounds had stopped.

"Tick most likely," I told her. "Go back to bed. I'll take care of it."

The door to Tick's room at the back of the house opened a ways and Jack stuck his head out.

"I got it," I said, waving him back.

He nodded and shut the door.

I picked up my boots at the bottom of the steps and carried them into the kitchen, leaving them by a chair there while I went out back in my stocking feet to take a quick look first.

Jack's hound was standing at the edge of the porch keeping a silent watch on things. When I come out, he pointed his long nose towards the car.

"What is it, Blue?" I asked, looking that way, which is when I spotted Tick's long legs sticking out the back door, his big flat feet on the ground.

"Well," I asked the dog, "should I wake him up or let him sleep it off?"

Blue looked up, squinting into the morning light.

"I know," I said. "Best let sleeping dogs lay, right?"

I turned and went back inside the house as Blue circled his rug—the one Ma had give him—and laid back down. I give some thought to going back to bed but decided I'd be better off to stay up since I would have to get up early for work anyway. I put a pot of coffee on the stove and set down at the table to wait on it to boil. Not five minutes later, Ma come padding her way in from down the hall.

"Where's your brother?" she asked me soon as she got in the kitchen.

"Out in the car," I answered.

"What's he doing there?"

"Sleeping it off, most likely."

"He'll freeze," she said.

"Not with all the alcohol he's likely got in his radiator," I said, grinning.

"Not funny," she said.

"Alright," I told her, "I'll go out and get him if you'll pour us some coffee."

"Thank you, son," she said, patting me on the arm.

"You sure you're ready to have him in the house?" I asked her as I slipped on my boots.

"He's still my son," she answered.

I got up out of the chair and headed back outside to get him, but by the time I got there, he was gone.

From the porch, I could see the car door still open where he'd been laying down in the back seat, but when I went to check, he was nowhere to be found.

"Where'd he go?" I asked the hound, then went back inside to let Ma know I was going out to look for her son again.

I took the car and drove around Pineville for the better part of an hour that morning, circling near every block in town, but I didn't find him.

I'm ashamed to say it now, 'specially after what happened later on, but the truth is I got plain tired of looking for him and threw up my hands. I drove back to the house to clean up for work and get a little something to eat, then headed over to the courthouse.

Before going to the Sheriff's Office, though, I checked the jail to be sure Tick hadn't got picked up wandering around town someplace. I thought maybe one of the city police officers might've come upon him staggering down some side street or back alley, but they hadn't, so I went on over to the office.

Floyd was already there, of course.

"Mornin', Sheriff," he said as I walked through the door.

"Mornin', Floyd," I groaned, not meaning to.

"Ever'thin' alright?" he asked, frowning.

"Whaddya mean?"

"You look a little wore out this mornin', that's all."

"I didn't get much sleep," I admitted.

"How'd it go over in Harlan yesterday?" he asked me.

"Why?" I asked, almost barking at him.

He looked startled. "I was only asking," he said like an apology.

"Sorry," I told him, "it ain't got nothing to do with you. I been up all morning looking for my brother is all."

"Your brother?"

"He's back in Pineville," I said without explaining how or why.

Floyd studied my face for a second, then asked if I wanted his help finding him. It was the kind of question that made me appreciate Floyd. No prying, no needing to be told the whole story, just him wanting to know if he could help. It made me want to try harder.

"I guess I ought to go back out looking again," I told him."I'd appreciate it if you'd stay and take care of things here again for awhile."

He nodded and I turned to go.

***

This time I started by making the rounds to places Tick might go to get a ride out of town. I went by the filling station at the corner of Pine, the bus station a block over from the Continental Hotel, and inside the hotel itself, where I fended off questions from Amos Sykes, the nosy clerk at the front desk.

"I'm just looking for somebody," I told him when he caught me walking through the lobby to the cafe.

"Anybody in particular?" he asked, giving me a suspicious look.

"Never mind," I told him, turning to leave.

"I seen your brother this mornin'," he told me as I headed for the door.

I stopped and spun back around.

"When?" I asked.

"I didn't know he was back in town," he said without answering the question. "Where's he been?"

I glared at him across the desk.

"Early," he answered, starting to look nervous behind the little reading glasses perched at the end of his pointed nose. "About daylight."

"He was here in the lobby?" I asked.

"No, I seen him out front, gettin' into a car with one of the reg'lars, a traveling salesman from up north. Leaves his automobile at the train station so he can make his rounds when he's here."

I thought for a second. "Was he comin' or goin'?"

"Your brother?" Amos asked.

"The salesman," I answered. "Did he check out?"

"I don't know. Let me look."

He turned around and run his finger across the pigeon holes behind him 'til he found the one he was looking for.

"Key's here and there's a check in the box," he told me, turning back around. "That means he's left for the week and most likely headed to the train station."

And that's how I learned where to go looking for my brother. For once, Amos Sykes' nosiness was worth the bother.

At the station, I found out Tick had bought a ticket for Lexington.

"Yessir," the station agent told me, "a feller fitting that description bought a ticket just this morning. Right after sunup it was. Sold him the ticket myself. He ain't runnin' from the law, is he?"

I didn't know how to answer but thanked him for his help and told him not to worry about it unless he seen him again.

"You'll let me know?" I asked, and he nodded.

From there, I went back by the house to tell Ma.

She frowned but didn't look too upset to find out he was gone, almost like she was expecting it.

"He'll be back when it suits him," I said, "or whenever he gets hisself into trouble again."

I didn't know then how right I was.

***

When I come back home for supper that evening after finishing up at the Sheriff's Office, the boy and his hound was both gone. I hadn't noticed it earlier when I come to tell Ma about Tick because I'd come in the front and left the same way right after.

"Where's Jack?" I asked Ma when I walked into the kitchen off the back porch.

"Left out right after breakfast this morning," she answered from the stove. "Said he needed to get going."

"Get going where?" I asked.

"Said he was going out to Curtis Philpot's place in Jenson."

"On foot?" I asked. "He say anything about his truck?"

"Didn't say nothing about a truck," she told me without turning around.

"How long's he been gone?"

"Got up right after you left this morning and said he was going to Jenson, that's all. I give him a poke full of ham biscuits to take with him."

"That don't sound right," I said, shaking my head, which is when I noticed the odd look on her face.

I set down and watched her go back and forth putting food on the table and pouring coffee. She wouldn't look at me.

"This was your idea, weren't it?" I finally asked her.

"Whatever are you talking about?" she answered, turning away to go put the coffee pot back on the burner.

"You *told* him to leave, didn't you?"

She didn't turn around.

"Ma?"

"What if them gun thugs from Harlan come looking for him?" she said with her back still turned.

"Well, it ain't like *me*-Curt lives on the moon," I told her. "They might find him there too, you know."

"Might as well be the moon, far back in the holler as Curtis is," she declared, finally turning around.

I had to grin.

"Wily old hen, ain't ya?" I said.

"You watch how you talk about your ma," she warned, wagging a finger in my direction, but she didn't deny it.

CHAPTER 7

GRACE GREATER THAN OUR SIN

About a week after Jack run off to my cousin Curtis' place after leaving our house and Tick run off to Lexington on the L&N line, me and Floyd come back in the office from serving a warrant and found a note from the switchboard telling me to call Agent Schilder again at the Bureau of Investigation in Cincinnati.

We'd been up in Arjay most of the day, in the cold, looking to serve a warrant on a man accused of dynamiting a splash dam upstream of the big sawmill there. I took Floyd with me on account of expecting trouble. I was told the man done it out of spite after being fired for fighting on the job and threatening to do bodily harm to the mill boss who fired him. But it was a wasted trip as it turned out. The man got wind of the warrant for his arrest and took off for Indian Mountain and a town called Jellico down in Tennessee, at least according to his pa. The poor old feller allowed as how his boy "always has been a hothead" and swore to let us know if ever he showed up in Arjay again.

"A day or two in jail wouldn't hurt him a bit," the old man told me. I didn't bother telling him his son would most likely get prison time for dynamiting a dam.

Anyhow, I was in a foul mood after that and finding the message to call Schilder when I got back in the Sheriff's Office didn't make it no better.

"Did the agent say what this was about?" I asked Verda when she come on the line.

"No, Sam," she said, "he just said to have you call him first chance you got."

"Alright, well, get him on the phone for me then," I told her and waited.

The first words out of Agent Schilder's mouth when he come on the line was, "It's about your brother," so I told him to hold on.

"Verda?" I said, then listened. But she must've already clicked off the line, so I told Schilder, "Okay, go ahead," without explaining.

"I'm sorry to be the one to have to tell you this, Sam," he said after that, and that's all it took before sorrow and regret gripped my heart like a vice. The rest of it I heard like I was under water: "Found dead in Cleveland . . . police searching . . . two suspects . . . 'Black Hand' gang . . . sorry as I can be . . . ." After clawing my way back to the surface, I started asking questions and learned that my brother was found face down in a dirt alley with two bullets in his back. The police didn't know who he was, so they took a picture of him laying on a slab in the morgue and sent it out to all the Bureau offices across the Midwest, one of which made its way to Schilder's desk.

"One of my men recognized Billy and brought the photograph to me," he said, "and that's when I called you. I didn't want just anybody calling you—or your ma."

I thanked him, for Ma's sake in particular, and at the end he surprised me by offering what he called "the government's assistance" in getting my brother's body shipped home to us from Cleveland.

"It's the least we can do, Sam, after all we put you through last summer" he said, meaning using me and Tick to get at the bootleggers and gangsters in Newport, which ended up getting us near killed in the bargain.

When I put down the phone, I felt empty. I'd been expecting a bad end for my brother for some time, but I weren't ready when it finally come. I got up and walked out to where Floyd was setting at his desk, telling him only that I needed to go home for something.

After that I went out back, got in the car, and drove to the house, where I parked out on the street and set behind the wheel for what seemed like the longest time 'til I worked up the nerve to climb them steps, go inside, and break Ma's heart.

***

Two days after Agent Schilder offered to ship my brother's body home for burial, I got a call at the office from a L&N freight agent saying it would be coming on the morning train from Lexington, which I found ironical since that's where Tick was headed the last time he left Pineville.

I asked Floyd to drive me to the station in his truck so I'd have a way to get it to the house.

"I s'pose we'll be alright to wait here," I told him as we pulled up to the loading dock around ten o'clock, when the train was expected.

He shut off the engine and I went inside. Not seeing anybody, I headed out on the platform where I found a old man in a work apron marking shipping crates with a piece of white chalk.

"What can I do fer ya?" he asked without stopping his work as I walked up.

"I'm here to pick up a shipment from Lexington," I told him, pointing back through the warehouse at Floyd's pick-up to make it clear to him.

"Train's running late," he told me as he went on with his scribbling.

"What time's it due?" I asked.

"Ought to be pulling in any minute," he answered, and right then a whistle blowed on the far side of the river.

"That'd be her," he told me, looking up for the first time and seeing my badge.

"What kind of shipment?" he asked, furrowing his brow.

"It's my brother," I told him.

He shook his head like he didn't understand. "Your brother?"

"His casket," I said, "my brother's casket."

"Oh," he answered, then stooped over to pick up a clipboard he'd laid down on top of the last box he marked.

After flipping through the pages, he said, "I don't see it here."

"I got a call about it at the courthouse," I told him, "just this morning,"

"Must be a special shipment then," he said, after which we stood on the platform together, silently watching the train's engine drag its load of cars across the river and into the station. From where we stood, it looked like a

long, black snake spewing white smoke from its nose.
When it got close, it let out a hiss of boiling steam and
slowed to a crawl, coming to rest with a jerk and a gasp at
the end of the terminal.

The old man stepped forward and slid open the heavy
door on the first freight car.

"It'll be in here if it's anywhere," he told me, and I followed him in to look among the barrels and crates stacked
up around the sides.

"That it?" I asked, pointing to a wooden box on the
floor.

It was knee high and seven or eight feet long but could
just as well have been a crate for shovels for all I could
tell.

I stepped up to take a closer look in the dim light of the
car. Across the top, somebody had scrawled **GARRETT/
Pineville/F.O.B.** in white chalk.

"What's FOB?" I asked.

"Free onboard shipping," the old man answered.
"Somebody high up took care of this one. Must be a
mighty fine casket. You gonna need help moving it to the
truck?"

"No," I told him as I waved Floyd over, "we can handle it."

"They's a cart by the office," he offered. "I'll get it for
you."

When he brung it back, I thought to tell him my
brother was inside that crate but somehow never got
around to it.

***

The viewing was set for that same evening, so we took the crate and all straight to the house from the station.

"Drive down the alley and back up to the porch," I told Floyd when we got close.

My plan was to pry the rough boards away from Tick's coffin, slide it off the back of the pick-up onto the dog's old rug there on the porch, and pull it like a mule sled through the kitchen to the living room.

Livie was already there, setting up the kitchen for when folks arrived with their casserole dishes and such, and caught us in the act. She was standing at the sink when we first come in and had her back to us.

"Sam," she said without turning around, "your ma needs to see you before you leave," but the sound of us sliding the heavy load across the floor must've got her attention.

When she turned and seen us wrestling with the casket, her mouth dropped open.

"What in the world are you doing?" she asked.

"Only way to get it here on time," I answered as we scooted it through. "Where's Ma?"

"Upstairs getting ready," she told me before I disappeared down the hall.

Deacon Locke, the long-faced widower from our church, was in Ma's parlor, helping set it up for the receiving. I was surprised to see him but grateful to have his help, even though he was a old man of near sixty at the time.

"Can you give us a hand here, Deacon?" I asked him, and after we turned the corner into the living room, he helped us heft the casket up on the table—the one I'd brung in from the dining room the night before.

Deacon Locke left the house after that to go back to his place and change clothes, and I headed back out through the kitchen with Floyd for him to to drive me back to the courthouse to get my car.

Livie caught me as we started out the back door.

"Did you go up and see your ma?" she asked.

"Plumb forgot," I told her, shaking my head.

I told Floyd I'd be out in a minute, then turned to go back down the hall.

Upstairs, I knocked on Ma's door.

She answered and I stepped inside. I found her setting at her vanity dresser in a house dress, combing out her hair.

"Livie said you wanted to see me?"

"I laid some clothes out on your brother's bed for you," she said.

"I'll get dressed when I get back from the Sheriff's Office," I told her, confused about why she'd be laying out clothes for me.

"Not for *you* to wear," she answered, looking back at me through the dresser's mirror, "for your brother."

I stared at her reflection 'til it come to me what she meant.

"Oh," I said. "I'll take care of it right now."

Downstairs, I laid out the white dress shirt, tie, and suit pants from Tick's room on a chair beside his casket, then run out to the truck to ask Floyd to give me another few minutes.

"Won't take long," I told him without saying what it was for and started back in as he took out the makings for a smoke.

Livie was waiting for me when I got back to the living room.

I stepped up to open my brother's coffin for the first time and was surprised to find him covered head to toe by a sheet of white linen. I reached out to take it down from his face, but froze up.

Livie touched my arm. "Let me help with that, Sam," she said in her softest voice. "I'm used to it."

I nodded and stood aside while she pulled the sheet down to his waist. The ashen color of his skin sent a shiver up my spine.

"Hand me his shirt," Livie said, breaking the uneasy silence.

She slid the right sleeve onto his right arm, then rolled his body away from her, like a patient at the hospital.

"Hold him," she said, slipping the rest of the shirt underneath as I kept him from rolling back on it.

"Now pull him towards you," she told me.

I rolled him my way 'til she got the shirt out from under him, then laid him slowly back down for her to slip the other sleeve on the opposite arm.

I picked up the pants and tie.

She buttoned his sleeves and the front of his shirt as I stood looking down at my brother's bloodless face.

"What is it?" she asked, seeing that I was in a daze.

"It's like when Pa died," I told her. "I stood by his coffin like this, watching him for the longest time. I stood there 'til I started to think he might open his eyes again if we could just wait long enough. I cried when they pulled me away to shut the lid."

"You go on, Sam," she said, reaching out to take the necktie from my hand. "I'll finish here."

"No," I told her. "I want to do it."

***

When I got back from the courthouse with the car, we already had a house full of people and a kitchen full of casseroles and cakes. I changed quick as I could and got back down to help Deacon Locke usher folks in.

Visitation wore on through the evening with mostly men and women from the church coming by to pay their respects. After a time, they settled down to talking about their troubles in life—aches and pains, debts and debtors, in-laws and the like—to the point where you'd think they forgot the reason we was all there. And none of the folks who stopped at Ma's chair to take her hand and tell her how sorry they was let on they had any idea what had happened to my brother, even if they'd heard the rumors. Like most folks in these parts, they knowed better than ask them kinds of questions.

The womenfolk chatted with one another while the men headed out to the kitchen for a bite to eat and a cup of coffee or glass of tea before going out on the back porch to smoke or chew. Then the mission ladies cleaned the dishes and put up the leftovers so Ma wouldn't have to cook for the next few days.

Ma stayed in the parlor talking to some late-comers while the others was busy in the kitchen. Eventually, they put on their coats and stopped by her chair to say their goodbyes and "bless yous" before heading back to their own homes.

Livie was the last one to leave. I would've drove her home myself, but she had Red's old car and was likely just as glad to have some peace and quiet at home by herself after all she'd done for Ma and me that afternoon (and after working her regular morning shift at the hospital too, I found out later).

Ma and me was both wore out. She went up to her room while I took a last smoke out on the back porch. I went to bed after that but laid awake staring at the ceiling, my fingers laced behind my head. I tried my best to stop thinking about my brother's last day alive, but it weren't no use. All I could think about was him running scared, being chased down and shot in the back, then taking his last breath on God's green earth with nobody there to care. I wanted to tell him I was sorry—sorry for his pain and sorry I weren't there to do nothing for him.

I don't know what time I finally did fall asleep, but I woke up early the next morning all the same. I put on a pair of pants and went to the toilet, then walked barefoot down the stairs so as not to wake Ma on my way to the kitchen. A gray fog thick as a storm cloud had rolled in off the river overnight, surrounding the house and unnerving me as I walked past my brother's dark casket in the living room.

I tip-toed past, down the hall, and switched on a light when I got to the kitchen, startled to find Ma setting up at the table in her housecoat, her dark hair down around her shoulders and her care-worn hands crossed on the table in front of her. But these days her hair was streaked through with gray, her hands spotted and veiny. I hadn't noticed 'til then how much she'd aged since me and my brother was boys.

"What're you doing up, Ma?" I asked her.

"Couldn't lay awake in bed no longer," she told me.

"You been awake all this time?"

"All but a hour or two. You want me to make you something to eat?"

"I couldn't eat right now," I told her.

"Alright," she said, and we looked at each other for what seemed like a long time before I turned to go back upstairs, forgetting all about whatever it was I come down for.

***

Later that morning, after we'd got dressed for the burial service, two thick-necked men in overalls showed up to the house in a delivery truck and parked out front. I met them at the door, where they announced they'd been sent by the Pineville Cemetery people to pick up my brother's coffin.

We hadn't paid for a funeral service, only the burying, so I didn't bother saying we was hoping for something more along the lines of a hearse with men dressed in coats and ties to lead us out to Billy's grave site. Instead, I asked if it would make it easier on them to pull 'round to the alley, where they could back up to the porch, but they told me they'd just as soon take it out the front, so I held the screen door for them while just the two of them, one on either end, carried my brother's coffin down the steps like a chifferobe or a chest of drawers. After they pulled away, I went back in to get my coat and walk Ma out to the car and drive her to the cemetery.

We didn't talk about the burial on the way but was satisfied that the grave was dug and Billy's coffin in it by the time we got there.

Other folks started showing up now that the sun was up over Pine Mountain and burning off the last of the morning fog. I.D., Chief Helton, and Judge Newsom and their wives was all there. Verda and just about every clerk in the courthouse come out for it too. Even old Amos Sykes come by to offer his condolences. Friends of Ma's and members of the church showed up, of course, the Lottie Moon mission ladies, in particular.

Livie was there in her nurse's uniform, as she had to work her shift at the hospital right after that and wouldn't have time to change. She was discomfited by it and wore a long winter coat during the service, but she looked just fine to me and I doubt anybody else even noticed.

We all stood together around the foot of my brother's grave while Reverend Pursiful read from the bible and talked about life and death and loss. Then we sung "In the Sweet By and By" and recited the Lord's Prayer before folks paraded by Ma to pay their last respects, each one reaching out to take her hand and gently pat it as they left.

After they was all gone, leaving only me and Livie and Ma standing around the grave, Ma said, "Pauline's gonna be awful put out with us, you know. Mammy will understand, but Pauline will have a fit when she finds out we didn't tell her."

"I can run out there and bring her back here if you want," I told her.

"I don't know," Ma said, "maybe in a day or two. That would be fine, I think."

I stood looking down into the open grave with my hands in my pockets with nothing to say.

"I hate it happened this time of year," Ma said, gazing around the cemetery. "There's no flowers this time of year. Nothing's blooming. We had cut flowers for Pa's grave when he died."

"We can bring some flowers at Easter for both of them," Livie offered, stepping over to Pa's headstone.

"Elias," she read from the top of the stone, then, pointing to the much smaller, hand-carved stone next to it, she asked, "Whose grave is this?"

"Mary's," I answered.

"That's the baby we lost," Ma told her. "Died of the fever, poor thing, before she could even walk. Sam was right around five year old then."

"Mary, Lamb of God," Livie read from the stone after bending down to study the weathered inscription.

"Pa carved that hisself," Ma told her. "Like to broke his heart when that baby died."

Livie reached out to trace the letters with her finger. "Poor little child," she said, "poor baby."

***

A day after Billy's burial, I left Floyd in charge of the Sheriff's Office and drove out to Stoney Fork to make amends with Pauline and Mammy for not coming out before that to let them know what happened to Billy—or even that he was dead.

I parked the car across the road from the swinging bridge and went to get a drink from the spring in the cleft of the rock like usual before crossing the road. As I sipped from the dipper, I thought about the times me and Tick had drunk from that spring as kids before racing each other across the road to the bridge while Ma hollered for us to watch for trucks, then yelled at us on the bridge to stop jumping up and down with her on it.

We'd run up the dirt path to the house, scattering chickens across the yard, then stomp up the porch steps to where Mammy set rocking in her chair the way she'd been doing since the beginning of the world so far as we knowed.

Pauline, Mammy's youngest who never seemed to age, played "cowboys and injuns" with us by helping us cut the bows and arrows from the limbs of saplings before running up and down the mountain with us, hiding behind rocks and trees and bushwhacking one another 'til we run our tongues out and come home to roost on the front porch again.

Then, after catching our breath, we'd play 'til near dark among the reeds and willows of the creek below the bridge, chasing dragonflies and other critters 'til the lightening bugs come out, then chasing them all the way back up the trail to the house again before it was time to get the "granny beads" washed out of our sweaty necks, the dirt scrubbed out of our ears, and the bottoms of our bare feet washed in time to get into bed, where we'd pick at one another 'til Ma had to come swat us on our behinds and tell us to settle down.

I was thinking about all that as I crossed the swinging bridge that day and looked up to find Pauline waving to me from the porch.

"Mammy said you might be coming to see us!" she told me when I got within earshot.

As I climbed the steps, I noticed Mammy's rocker was empty.

"She ain't sick, is she?" I asked.

"No, just got cold and come in by the fire," my aunt told me, "which is where we ought to be. It's wintertime up here in case you ain't noticed."

"Hold on, Pauline," I said before we started inside. "They's something I need to tell you first."

"Something wrong with Ev?" she asked, talking about my ma.

"No," I told her, "Ma's fine."

"Then what is it?"

I felt the weight of it on my heart of a sudden and changed my mind.

"It'll wait," I said, putting it off as long as I might.

Pauline give me a funny look but led the way inside to where Mammy was dozing by the fire.

"Look who's come to see us, Mammy!" Pauline said, waking her up.

Mammy looked up and smiled as I stepped close to pat her hand and kiss her wrinkled cheek.

"It's good to see you, Sam," she said, patting me back.

"I got something to tell you, Mammy," I said, working up my nerve again, "you and Pauline both."

But that's when I noticed Eugenia and the children at the kitchen table.

"Hello, Genia," I said, smiling. "How's them littl'uns doing?"

"They's both fine, Sam," she smiled back.

"I wonder if you might take them girls in the back for a little while? I got something I need to discuss with Mammy and Pauline."

Jack's sister didn't hesitate.

"Let's go play with your doll babies," she told the girls, then led them away by the hand.

Pauline set down by Mammy and I pulled up a chair from the kitchen.

"Now, what's this all about, Samuel Lee?" Pauline asked, narrowing her eyes and frowning.

I didn't waste no more time getting to the point, but I didn't tell everything I knowed neither, just the part about how Billy went off up north but ended up getting killed by some bad men. I didn't feel like they needed to know all that happened in between.

"Ain't you goin' after them men yourself?" Pauline asked me when I finished.

Taken aback by the question, I answered, "No, the law's looking for 'em."

"But he's our kin," Pauline said like I was forgetting a blood oath.

I struggled to make sense of it for her.

"I cain't go hunting men in places that ain't in my jurisdiction," I told her. "Besides, I don't know who they are."

I could see it in her face that she didn't understand.

"The Bible says 'a eye for a eye'," she reminded me, and that's when Mammy interrupted her.

"Leave the boy be, Pauline," she said, reaching out to touch her arm and quiet her the way Ma sometimes did me. "He cain't change what's foretold."

"Foretold?" Pauline asked.

I studied Mammy's face in the flickering light of the fire. "The buck," I said, remembering her story, "and the wolves."

"Catamounts," Mammy corrected me.

"Catamounts," I answered, nodding.

***

I left Mammy's feeling like a weight was lifted from my shoulders. Strange as it sounds, I was beginning to understand how them dreams, them visions of hers had a power I never understood before. They was more than forewarnings, they was a way of helping folks brace for whatever bad might happen in their lives—even if them things never come true.

I ain't saying I believe in predictions, but I believe in dealing the best way we can with whatever comes our way, which is roundabout way of explaining why I decided to stop by my cousin Curtis' place in Jenson on my way back from Stoney Fork that day.

I found him setting out front of his pole cabin, his back propped against one of the rough cedar posts holding up the roof over his porch. It was early afternoon and he was just setting out there in the sun, rolling a smoke. When I drove up, the 'baccer pouch was still dangling from between his teeth by its string while he folded the cigarette paper between his fingers.

I pulled up, got out, and stood at the front of the car with my hands in my pockets, watching and waiting.

"Fergit somethin'?" he asked after filling the paper, licking it, and rolling it closed.

"Maybe," I said.

"What?" he asked as he put the cigarette in his mouth.

That's when I noticed the half-empty mason jar next to his one remaining leg.

"You ain't moonlighting your own 'shine these days, are ya?"

"That what you come all the way out here to ask me?"

"No," I answered. "Is it any good?"

"Kisses like a woman and kicks like a mule," he grinned. "Want a swig?"

"Too early in the day," I told him, then waited for him to light his smoke and take a draw.

"You got a minute?" I asked when he was done.

"I don't know, *me*-Sam," he grinned after blowing the smoke out. "You can see I'm awful damn busy right now."

I smiled.

"What's on yer mind?" he asked. "This ain't about Jack Grimes again, I hope."

"Not really," I answered.

"Then what?" he asked.

"I s'pect you heard about Tick."

He nodded.

"Word travels fast through these hollers. How's your ma takin' it?"

"Well as can be expected, I s'pose."

"They got any idea who done it?"

"They got a pretty good idea, but it don't much matter, I reckon. What's done is done."

"Kind of like what happened with Dewey Grimes, then," Curtis said, seeming to figure out what I'd come to see him about.

"You been back up to Pickerin pond since then?" I asked.

"No, I ain't," he told me, peering through the cloud of smoke between us. "It's a long haul for a man with one leg."

"Maybe we ought to run up there in the car and take a look around," I said.

Curtis took another draw and let it out, all the while looking me in the eye.

"Now why in hell would you want to go stirring all that up again?" he asked.

I looked at the ground and dug the toe of my boot into the dirt.

"I doubt you'd tell me anyway," I answered, "if Jack was hiding out up there, I mean."

"I thought this weren't about Jack," he reminded me.

"Well," I said as I stopped digging in the dirt and looked up again, "what if I said I wouldn't much care if he was?"

"Then I'd say he'd be right glad to hear it," Curtis answered with a sly grin.

"Well, you know," I told him, "after I get swore in as sheriff, I'll be needing to spend more time at the court-house. I won't be out running around in the county so much like I been doing."

"That's too bad," he said. "I'll miss you comin' 'round to visit."

"And you'll tell Jack? If you see him, I mean."

"I will," he nodded, "if'n I do."

"Alright, then," I said, turning to leave, "you take care of yourself, *me*-Curt, you hear?"

"You too, *me*-Sam," he answered.

CHAPTER 8

MURDER CREEK

It weren't but a day after I'd been out to Stoney Fork to see Mammy and Pauline and then on to Jenson to see cousin Curtis that I got another call from Lester Ball, the Harlan County jailer.

"I thought you'd want to know," he said right off the bat, "Jim Jenkins is dead."

"Devil Jim?" I asked.

"Is there another?"

"I hope not," I said.

"He turned up dead here about a week ago. I thought you'd want to know."

"What happened?"

"Hung hisself. At least that's what the coroner's report says."

"That'd take a mighty strong rope," I told him.

"I reckon!" Lester agreed.

"Where'd it happen?" I asked. "Was he still in jail?"

"No, the 'sociation bailed him out," Lester told me. "He was found hanging from a low limb of a sycamore tree out at Murder Creek."

"Murder Creek?"

"I know," he said, "ironical, ain't it?"

"Wait a minute," I said. "Didn't you just say Devil Jim was out on bail when this happened?"

"That's right."

I shook my head, wondering what the hell had gone on there.

"How's a man get bail after killing a woman?" I asked. "I don't care if he is a deputy, that ain't how we do things in Bell County."

"Jim was charged with *shootin'* Big Sal, Sam, if that's what you mean. She ain't *dead!*"

"Ain't dead? But I seen her myself, laying right there on the cellar steps."

"Naw," the jailer snorted, "the docs at the hospital brung her around. It'd take more'n one slug in her hip to do in a woman like Big Sal, don't you think?"

"Well, I'll be damned!" I said, smiling to myself.

"And you might be too," he told me, "if you ever show your face in the *Corner Cafe* again."

"And why's that?" I asked.

"'Cause she told me she heard you call her 'Big Sal' that day when they was carrying her out on a stretcher, that's why!"

I laughed, then asked him something else I'd wondered about that day.

"You ever find out how she come to be at the courthouse that morning? I mean, how come her to be there the exact same time as Devil Jim—and carrying a pistol?"

"Damndest thing," he told me. "She'd come looking for me to show her how to reload it, of all things. The cylinder was jammed and that was the last bullet in it, the one she ended up using on Jim!"

"But why'd she go to the cellar?" I asked.

"Oh, that," he said. "Told me she just happened to walk in behind 'em when Jim had Boyd at gunpoint out in the hall. She followed 'em down there without them even knowing it. Now, ain't that something?"

"You really think Devil Jim hung hisself, though?" I asked.

"No, and neither does Boyd. He says the 'sociation done it. Says they only bailed Jim out to shut him up on account of him gettin' too big for his britches and threatening to tell what he knowed if they didn't get him out of jail and pay him to keep his mouth shut about what all they been doin' here."

"Serves him right, I s'pose."

"I s'pose," Lester said. "By the way, whatever become of your brother?"

"Nothing good," I told him, wondering how much I wanted to say about that. Then, "It's like Boyd said," I told him, "he 'made his bed' and it caught up with him. He ain't around no more."

"Sorry to hear it," Lester said, likely not knowing what I meant by that. "And what become of the boy?—the one that lets his hound drive his truck."

"*Jack*," I reminded him. "He's gone back to the holler he come from—him and his dog both. Which reminds me, you still got that truck of his?"

"Sure," Lester answered. "It's out at Boyd's place, parked in the barn. If you see the boy, you can tell him he can come get it anytime he wants."

"Maybe I'll send somebody around for it one day soon," I told him, "if that'd be alright."

"Sure, Sam, anytime," he answered.

We both run out of things to say, I reckon, and got quiet.

"Anyhow," Lester said after a little, "I just thought you'd want to know what become of Devil Jim after all the trouble he caused."

"I 'preciate it," I said.

"Well, don't be a stranger," he told me, and we hung up.

CHAPTER 9

LIVIE AND RED

A round of sickness hit Bell County right around Thanksgiving that year, causing Livie to have to work extry shifts without much notice and pretty much ruining Ma's plans for cooking a big dinner and inviting her and her pa to join us at the house. It was Ma's idea for me to call Livie at the hospital early on a Sunday we knowed she was working the morning shift and invite her to come to the house after church for supper.

"Hard as that girl works, she could likely use some home cooking," Ma told me, so I called for her from the house that morning.

"Can you get Livie Brock on the phone for me?" I asked the nurse at the desk. "She's on duty this morning."

"Hold the line," she said.

Then, less than a minute later, she come back on to tell me Livie weren't there.

"You sure?" I asked.

"I called ever' floor," she told me.

"She's s'posed to be working," I said, mostly to myself.

"Who's this?" she asked.

"Sam Garrett," I answered.

"Oh, you're Livie's fella, ain't ya? Let me check the schedule."

I heard papers being shuffled, then she come back on the line to say, "She was scheduled, but somebody's marked through it."

"Did she change her shift?" I asked, bothered that she'd forgot to tell me if she did.

"There's no note nor nothin'," she told me. "I can find out and get back to you, but I can't leave the desk. Ain't nobody else here right now."

"No, that's alright," I told her.

"I can leave a note for her if you want," the nurse offered.

"No," I said again, "thanks anyway."

I was just hanging up when Ma come in the kitchen from upstairs after changing out of her church clothes.

"You might drive over to the hospital and pick Livie up, Sam," she said. "She'll be wore out."

"She ain't there," I said as Ma tied her apron on.

I was about to explain it to her when the telephone rung.

"Hello?" I answered.

"Who's this?" a gruff voice on the other end demanded to know.

It was Doc Slusher. I recognized his bark.

"Sam Garrett," I answered. "Sheriff Atkins' deputy."

"Well this is Willard Slusher," he said as if I didn't know. "The nurse here tells me you called for Olivia Brock?"

"A couple of minutes ago," I told him. "She's supposed to be working this morning, and I—"

"I sent her home," he said, cutting me off.

"Sent her home?"

"That's right. Can't have her in with the patients, so I sent her home."

"She sick?" I asked.

"Ain't that what I just said?" he growled.

"What is it, Sam?" Ma asked from behind me.

I held my hand over the mouthpiece.

"Doc Slusher says he sent Livie home sick from the hospital."

"Did he say what's wrong with her?"

"I was just about to ask him," I said, going back to the call, but the line was dead.

"He hung up."

"Maybe you should drive out to the house and check on her," Ma suggested.

"I might," I told her as I hung up the earpiece. "I'll try calling first."

Nobody answered the ring, so I drove out there, still dressed in my church clothes, and found Red setting out on the front porch in his usual chair. His car was parked in the front yard.

"Sorry, Sam," Red told me after I explained why I was there. "I might've been bringing her in the house about that time. I didn't hear any telephone ring."

"That's alright," I said. "S'pose I can see her now that I'm here?"

"She's covered up to her chin in blankets and got the shades pulled," he told me, "but you can go in and see if she's awake."

I went in, knocked at the door, and called her name.

She answered in a voice so weak and thin I could hardly hear her.

"Sam?"

"Can I come in?" I asked, opening the door a crack.

"No, don't come in," she said is a raspy whisper. "I might be contagious. They sent me home from the hospital."

"I know," I told her through the crack. "I talked to Doc Slusher. You need anything?"

"Some water," she answered, then coughed like her throat hurt.

I turned to go fetch a glass from the kitchen but found Red standing behind me when I did.

"She's been like that since I got her home," he told me. "She'll have a coughing fit, ask for water, then fall off to sleep by the time I get back with it."

"They say what's wrong with her?" I asked.

"No, just said to come get her. It weren't but a hour after I'd dropped her off this morning."

"You been driving her?"

"Had to. They been working her all hours here lately and the bus don't run but twice't a day."

"She had anything to eat?" I asked.

"No. She won't take nothing. I tried. What's the matter with her, you reckon?"

"I don't know," I told him, "but I'm fixin' to find out soon as I can catch up with Doc Slusher. I'll call you when I know something. Anything else you need?"

"Can you bring her some aspirins?" Red asked. "I mean, if you're a'comin' back later. She asked for 'em when I got her home, but they's nary a one in the house, and I don't want to leave her here on her own to go get any."

"Sure thing," I told him as I turned to leave.

We walked through the house together and was at the front door by the time I remembered the water.

"Wait," I said, "I forgot to get her a glass of water."

"You go on," Red told me. "I'll get it. Pump's been acting up here lately and might take a minute to clear. She's not likely to be awake to drink it by then anyhow."

"Well, you know how to get hold of me," I told him as I started out the door and down the steps. "I'll let you know what I find out and when I can get back here with them aspirins."

"Thanks for comin' out, Sam," he said.

Red followed me out on the porch and watched me all the way to the car. I still sometimes think about the worried look on his face as I pulled away from the house that morning.

***

I drove straight to the hospital looking for Doc Slusher after that, but the nurse at the desk told me I'd just missed him.

"He's finished making his rounds," she said, "but you might catch him at his office. He usually goes there before he goes home."

I hurried across the street and found him out on the sidewalk in front of his office, fussing with the door latch. As I walked up, I could see he was struggling to fit his key into the lock.

"Here, let me help with that," I said, stepping in beside him.

He handed it over without a argument, which was surprising.

"Got to get that damn lock replaced one of these days," he complained as I slipped the key into the lock with no problem.

"Seems okay to me," I said as I unlocked the door and opened it for him.

"You here for a reason?" he asked, pushing his wire-rim glasses back up on his nose to look at me.

"I come to ask you a question," I said, standing back so he could go in first. "I just come from Livie's place out at Fourmile, and . . ."

He stopped short and turned around, causing me to trail off before I finished.

"Olivia?" he asked.

I nodded.

"That was a damn fool thing to do," he barked at me. "I sent her home for a reason. She's supposed to be kept in quarantine."

"Quar'ntine?" I asked.

"She was exposed to diphtheria at the hospital," he told me as he turned back around.

I followed him through the darkened waiting room to his office in back.

"Ain't that something chil'un get?" I asked, remembering having heard about it from Ma.

"That's right," he told me as we walked in the office, "but Olivia's not that much older than some of the children she's been tending to."

He switched on a light on his desk, took off his doctor's coat, and hung it on a rack in the corner. Then he pulled a pair of half glasses out of his shirt pocket and changed them out for the glasses he had on.

I handed him his door key and he laid it on the desk before turning to a shelf to pick up a thick gray medical book, which he opened on top of his desk. He used his forefinger to pick out one of the little black tabs that run down the outside of the pages and thumbed through 'til he found what he was looking for.

"Here it is," he said, bending over to get close to the page.

"What is it?" I asked as he read.

He looked up like he'd forgot I was there, then went back to the book, muttering to hisself: "Swollen lymph nodes, a white patch in the back of the throat . . . of course, that white patch could be thrush, but with the other symptoms . . . "

"Red said she had chills and a fever," I told him, trying to help. (I stopped short of telling him I'd heard Aunt Pauline say Mammy could cure the thrush by blowing in your mouth, but I didn't really think he'd care to hear that.)

He stopped and looked up at me over the top of his glasses.

"Who's Red?" he asked.

"Her pa," I told him. "Red Brock."

"Oh," he said, looking back down at the book.

"Ain't diphtheria kinda dangerous?" I asked while I had his attention.

He shook his head. "It can be—in young children—but Olivia ought to recover once the fever breaks."

"Ain't they nothing you can give her for it?" I asked.

"Aspirin and bed rest," he answered, closing the book. "That's about it."

"That ain't much to go on," I said.

"Well, if her fever don't break in a couple of days, have her pa call me—here or at the hospital."

"I can run you out to her house right now," I offered.

"No," he answered, "have him call me if the fever doesn't break."

I left the doc's office no better off than when I got there as far as helping Livie was concerned, but at least now I had some idea what was wrong with her.

***

When I got home, Ma was getting ready to go to evening services at the church. She was in the kitchen, already dressed but still in her apron, putting up dishes she'd washed.

"I talked to Doc Slusher," I told her, taking the plate she was drying and putting it away in the cupboard.

"And what'd he say?" she asked as she untied her apron to take it off.

"Says it might be diphtheria."

"I thought only young'uns got that," she said, folding the apron to lay it across the empty dish rack on the sink.

"He says it ain't likely for somebody her age, but she's plenty sick, whatever she's got."

Ma went to the table and set down in one of the chairs, laying her hands in her lap.

"What did he say do for her?" she asked me, frowning.

"Said she needs bed rest and aspirins."

"That's all?"

"That and to call him if the fever don't break soon. But Red told me they ain't got any aspirins."

"That don't sound good, Sam. Red's all alone and might need help with her."

I nodded and moved over to the wall phone.

"I'll let him know we're coming," I said.

"I'll go up and get a bottle of aspirins," Ma offered. "I won't be a minute."

I rung up the city operator, but after three tries calling out to Fourmile and getting no answer, she asked what I wanted to do.

"I can keep trying and call you back if I get him," she offered.

"No, that's alright," I told her. "I'm headed that way now."

By then Ma was back downstairs and in the kitchen.

"Red don't answer," I told her as I hung up the earpiece.

"Maybe he's busy with Livie."

"I reckon," I said.

"I was thinking . . ."

"What?" I asked her.

"Maybe we ought to pack up some leftovers to take out there with us."

"Why?"

"Livie ain't likely had nothing to eat," she answered. "Red neither, for that matter."

"We ain't got time for all that," I argued, but I was wasting my breath. Ma already had the icebox open by then.

To satisfy her, I helped wrap up a plate of ham and biscuits and carried them to the car, laying them on the floorboard at her feet after helping her in.

We drove out the back road by the river to save time.

In spite of the fall chill, I expected to find Red setting out on the porch like usual, but he weren't there. His car was still parked out front, but his chair was empty.

"I'll run up and knock," I told Ma.

"I'll wait here," she said.

But Red never come to the door. I hollered his name two or three times, then tried the latch. It was unlocked, so I let myself in. Inside, the front hall was cold and dark as a cave.

"Red?" I hollered again, but the echo of my own voice ringing through the house was all I heard back.

I went to Livie's room and pushed her door open a crack, calling out "Livie" in a loud whisper as I did, but she didn't answer.

The shades was drawn in the darkened room, so I made my way to a window to let in some light. When I turned back, I seen Livie laying face up on the bed, a ball of sheets and blankets wound around her, her arms and legs outstretched on either side.

I went to her and bent over to touch her shoulder but stopped with a shudder when I seen that both her eyes was wide open and fixed on the ceiling. I laid my hand on her forehead. She was burning up. Her ginger hair, wet and stringy, clung to her face. The pillow beneath her head was soaked.

I leaned closer to her ear and said her name. This time she moaned and mouthed "Sam," but it were like she was having a fever dream.

"Where's Red, Livie?" I asked her, talking louder now. "Where's your pa?"

A voice behind me called out "Sam" and I near jumped out of my skin. It was Ma.

"Is she alright?"

"No," I answered, standing back up and turning around. "Did her pa come out?"

"No," Ma answered, shaking her head.

"Stay in here a minute with her, will you?" I asked.

She nodded. "Where you going?"

"I need to find Red," I told her, "then get Livie to the hospital."

"Alright," Ma said, moving to the bed.

I went to look for Red again, this time passing through the kitchen and out the back door. I looked in the coal shed, then the tool barn, and finally even opened the door to the outhouse—everywhere and anywhere I could think of.

Not finding him, and remembering Livie had said his room was located up a steep staircase off the kitchen, I went back in the house, climbed the steps, pushed open the whitewashed board and batten door at the top, and found her pa laying on the floorboards between the foot of his bed and a dresser. His face was bloodless and pale as my brother's had been in his coffin.

I run back down to Livie's room.

"Red's gone," I told Ma.

She looked confused. "Gone where?" she asked, and I realized she thought I meant something different.

"He's dead, Ma," I said, hoping Livie weren't hearing this.

"You sure?" she asked, looking unsettled.

"Sure as rain," I told her as I went to lift Livie off the bed.

"What're you doing?"

"Taking Livie to the hospital, like I said."

"We can't just leave her pa here, can we?" she asked, wide-eyed.

"Can't be helped, Ma. He's upstairs and the two of us can't carry him. Bring one of them blankets off the bed to cover her with, alright?"

We didn't talk as we hurried out of the house and down the front steps towards the car.

I carried Livie across the yard in my arms, put her in the back seat with Ma, and drove fast as I dared over the rutted road back into town while she talked to Livie like she was her child—soothing her and stroking her hair.

At the hospital, I jumped out to carry her up the steps and inside, blanket and all.

"Careful, Sam," Ma told me as I pulled Livie from the back seat, and it was then I noticed she'd closed her eyes sometime during the ride.

When I got her into the lobby, a nurse I recognized—the one with glasses thick as the bottom of a *Coca-Cola* bottle—jumped up from her chair to open the door into the main hallway for us.

"Right through here," she told me, but she didn't need to. I'd been there back in the summer, with Jack Grimes' little sister.

Another nurse at the desk in the hall showed us into a empty room.

"I'll get the doc," she offered as I laid Livie down on the hospital bed.

About a minute after that, the same nurse come back in with Doc Slusher.

"Wait outside," he ordered me in his bulldog way.

The nurse took me by the arm and led me back out into the hall.

"We'll let you know," she said before going back in with the doc and closing the door.

I took a seat in a chair by the nurses' station but couldn't set still and got back up again, pacing back and forth 'til I decided to go out and get Ma.

She'd already got out of the car. I found her waiting in the lobby quiet as a church mouse, her hands clasped in her lap.

"What did they say?" she asked as I walked up to her chair.

"She's fine for now," I told her. "They've got her resting while they try and get the fever down."

"What can we do?" she asked.

"Nothing I know of," I answered.

I noticed then how tired she looked.

"Ma, you might as well be at home as here," I said. "Why don't you let me take you to the house?"

"I can stay if you need me," she offered.

"No," I told her, "let me check on Livie again, then I'll take you."

She nodded, giving in, and I went back to the nurses' station in the hall.

By then the doc was setting at the desk, filling out a chart.

I walked up and asked him how Livie was doing.

"We've got to get more fluids in her to get her temperature down," he told me, looking up from the chart. "The nurses will take care of that and I'll check on her again tomorrow."

"But why won't she wake up?" I asked him. "Her pa told me she ain't been doing nothing but sleeping since he brung her home from the hospital this morning."

"Is he here?" Doc asked, and I thought again of Red laying lifeless on the floor of his room.

"No," I told him and explained.

"Does Olivia know?" he asked.

"I don't think so."

"Do you want an ambulance?"

"What?"

"An ambulance," he repeated. "I can arrange one, but you'll need to go with them to pick him up."

***

In the end, I had the hospital ambulance follow me and Ma to our house first so I could let her out, then on to Livie's place at Fourmile. I had them park around the back by the kitchen door, and it didn't take no time a'tall after that for me and the two orderlies the doc sent to carry Red's body down the back stairs, get him onto the gurney, and load him into the back. I followed them back to the hospital, then inside to the morgue, where the doc had told me to wait for him. He showed up about the same time they got Red's body moved from the gurney onto a steel table.

"What would you estimate as the time of death?" Doc Slusher asked me as he leaned over Red's chest to listen in with his stethoscope.

"Can't say for sure," I told him, "sometime this afternoon."

"Your best guess then," he grumbled.

"Well, he was still alive when I drove out there a little after church this morning, so—"

"What time was that?"

"Around dinnertime, I reckon. He was settin' out on his porch and we talked. Then I went back out there after you and me talked in your office."

"After I told you Olivia was quarantined?"

"Well, yessir, but—"

"Never mind," he snapped. "What time was that?"

"Around suppertime," I answered, "not long before I showed up here with Livie."

He looked at his watch.

"So between four and six o'clock, then?"

"About that, I reckon."

"And was he cold to the touch when you found him?"

I nodded.

"Alright," he said, taking a pen from his pocket to scribble a note. "I'll have to do a more thorough examination, of course, but if I had to hazard a guess, I'd say this was a heart attack or stroke. I'll let you know if I find anything other than that—unless you think we ought to bring the coroner in on this for some reason."

"Uh, no," I answered right quick.

"Alright then," he said, turning back to the table.

"Thanks, Doc," I said and left him to his work.

***

That was that 'til I got to thinking about what to do about the funeral and burial for Red if Livie didn't get better soon, and that same evening, I drove out to Mill Creek to let the Brocks know what had happened.

I surely hated to be the one to bring them the bad news, but there was nobody else to do it. Red's brother was there with the rest of the clan, and I think they suspected something as soon as I showed up at the door, even though I was still dressed for church and not wearing my uniform shirt.

I eased into it by explaining about Livie and how I'd went out to Fourmile to check on her and ended up bringing her to the hospital, but then I had to tell them how I found Red upstairs in his room.

They took it pretty good, all in all, so then I offered to see about getting his body moved to wherever they wanted it moved to, but they allowed as how they'd take care of it theirselves, so I let that it go and we talked more about what was ailing Livie and what room she was in at the hospital and so on so they could go visit. I heard from the nurses later on that the Brocks had all come in at once to visit her and near shut down the whole floor on account of how many there was of them!

I run into the doc during his rounds early one morning on a visit of my own and learnt they'd come and got "Charles"—that was Red's Christian name—and took him back to Mill Creek to be laid to eternal rest in the family cemetery, but Livie still hadn't woke up by the day of the burial and missed it.

Then one day, like a miracle in the Bible, she woke up! I'd stopped by her room on my way to the courthouse like I'd done every morning since we first brung her there almost a week before and found her setting up in the bed pretty as you please.

"Well, ain't you a sight for sore eyes!" I told her, and she smiled back at me as big and bright as a summer sun.

It was the happiest day of my life up 'til then, I do believe—that is, 'til it hit me I'd have to be the one to break it to her about her pa.

EPILOGUE

Livie and me finally did get married, but it weren't on Christmas Day like she always said she wanted and it weren't in the church like Ma wanted. Instead, we decided to have what's called a "civil ceremony" before the bench the same day Judge Newsom swore me in as the new high sheriff of Bell County.

It weren't my idea, though, it were Livie's. We'd been out to Mill Creek to visit her pa's grave, where he was buried alongside her ma, Florence, and his ma and pa, John Henry and Saylor, and got to talking about how life is short and none of us knows when the next day might be our last, and . . . well, you know. So, anyway, we set the date.

We hadn't told too many folks what we was planning to do, so it was only the two of us and Ma, plus a smattering of others who'd come mostly for the swearing in. Livie wore her ma's brocade dress—the one she'd wore when her and Red got married—and I wore my new uniform. Ma was disappointed about the wedding part, but she took a lot of pride in my swearing-in ceremony and give us her blessing.

Virgil and I.D. was both there, of course, and signed as witnesses on the marriage certificate. Floyd come upstairs and brung Alvey with him from the jail, mostly just for the swearing in.

Verda come up from the switchboard, having got Lucybell to take over for her that morning, and sidled up to Livie like a pretend maid of honor for the marrying part, I noticed.

Virgil made a wisecrack about it being a good morning to rob the Pineville bank, "What with the sheriff taking time off to get married and all," he said, which kind of brings me around to what happened with Lovis Evans, the gap-tooth coroner.

Later that same year, Lovis took over from Virgil as Pineville's police chief, but after everything the mayor done to set him up in the job, the jackass up and quit only six months into it (just like Virgil predicted, if I remember right). What happened was, Lovis got found out "selling pardons" and ended up resigning to escape charges of official misconduct, accepting bribes, and misappropriation of funds, as the writ said.

The way it come about was this. Sometime around March or April of that same year, Alvey told Floyd (who told me) that some of the prisoners seemed to be getting out of jail ahead of time and it was Lovis who was signing off on turning them loose without due process. Now, even a ordinary fool ought to know a chief of police will get caught at a thing like that sooner or later, 'specially when word gets out that all a feller has to do is ransom hisself to the chief to go free, but I reckon Lovis was a special kind of fool, because he didn't even bother to cover his own tracks. He kept the money in his bank account, where it was easy to trace, so it didn't take long for the judge to get to the truth of it once it was pointed out to him what was going on. (I ain't saying who done the pointing out, but I might've let it slip a time or two that something "fishy" was going on over at the jail.)

That weren't the end of it, though, because Judge Newsom started digging in deeper after that and found out Lovis had been padding the city's bills to the county for care and feeding of them very same prisoners after he'd already let them out of jail! So that was another offense, and the judge give him the choice of resigning or facing criminal charges.

Lovis likely thought he'd got off easy by resigning as chief, but unbeknownst to him, Judge Newsom had already wrote a letter to the state regulators in Lexington recommending that they look into four or five years worth of reimbursements he submitted to the Commonwealth of Kentucky as the Bell County coroner.

Things only got worse for Lovis after that, and it didn't take long before the slippery weasel was up on charges of falsifying official records. Like the judge once said, Lovis Evans was the kind of feller who'd steal nickels and dimes out of a blind beggar's cup and count hisself clever for doing it.

Course, Lovis' people being big in politics in Bell County like they was, he never went to jail for none of his thievery and corruption, but it was gratifying as hell to see him have to resign his office and run back home to Middlesboro to hide.

The only bad thing about it was, I lost Floyd that summer to the City of Pineville when they offered him the chief of police job to replace Lovis. I hated like anything to see him go, but he left with my blessing. If anybody in the county deserved to profit from the mess Lovis and the mayor made, it was Floyd Clayburn.

***

The other thing that come about during this time was Virgil and Floyd traded houses, like Virgil said they might, and Virgil moved out to the Clayburn farm with the missus. Later on, Alvey and Verda got together, just like Virgil hoped, got married and offered to rent Red's place from Livie since she weren't living there and had no need of it. I took care of the back taxes on the place and Verda and Alvey moved in down the road from her ma and pa.

Livie and me had give some thought to moving into that house ourselves after we got married, but Ma talked us out of it, saying we could both stay close to our jobs in town if we stayed there with her. We had to admit it made good sense, so Livie and me took up married life right there at the house in Pineville.

But like I said before, Ma was a wily old hen and had tricks up her sleeve that I didn't have a clue about. Right after Livie and me got married, Ma started inviting Deacon Locke over for Sunday dinner pretty regular, and then one evening after church, she told us the two of them was getting married! I'd been blind to it the whole time, I guess, and had to have Livie point out to me that the two of them had been keeping regular company at church services and even at the movie house on Saturday afternoons, all right under my nose.

"Smiley" asked for my blessing to marry Ma, which was his way of saying he cared what I thought, I s'pose, and it weren't long after that they got married in the church and moved into his place off Kentucky Avenue, leaving Ma's house to me and Livie, and the two of us started planning a family.

Turned out Livie and me wouldn't have no babies of our own, though. After a year or two of trying, she went to Doc Slusher without telling me and got him to do some tests that showed she was barren—most likely caused by the sickness she'd had, he told her, not to mention the upset of losing her pa at the same time. I was always more sorry for her than I ever was for myself about not having children. She was down on herself about it for a long time but then throwed herself into her nursing work and got a lot of satisfaction out of helping other folks' littl'uns. She even worked with Doc Slusher to set up the county's first board of health through Judge Newsom's court, something Bell County hadn't even thought of doing before that, and the judge come up with the money she needed to go out to schools in the county and help children in the lumber and mining camps, inoculating them against diphtheria and all manner of diseases and learning them and their folks about hygiene and the like.

A lot of times, I'd take her out in the sheriff's car to help convince the parents they ought to do the right thing by their children. I even drove her out to Mammy's in Stoney Fork one day, though it was rightly Pauline's place by then on account of Mammy had gone to glory by then. Anyway, I took Livie out there to inoculate them two littl'uns of Genia's. I can still hear Pauline throwing a fit.

"You ain't gonna stick that needle in them poor chil'un's arms, are ya?" she cried, near beside herself. "They ain't even sick!"

***

I never had call to go back to Harlan that first year after I become sheriff, but I read plenty about it. I'd started taking their paper through the mail to keep up with the goings on there, since I knowed the jailer and his brother Boyd, not to mention Big Sal. Mostly, though, I wanted to keep up with which side was getting the upper hand between the mining companies and the miners union. Seemed to me whatever was happening there might work its way into Bell County sooner or later and it might do me good to keep up with it.

It weren't long after the new sheriff took over from Boyd Ball in January that some of the union men started striking against the mining companies, and it had a lot to do with Sheriff Blair taking the side of the companies every time, just like Lester said he would.

One day in early May, almost five months to the day after I become sheriff, a few of the UMWA men in Evarts got fed up and took potshots at some Baldwin-Felts gun thugs and sheriff's deputies who was escorting "scabs" into the mines there. Scabs, I learnt, is what they call strike breakers hired by the company to replace union men, and the newspaper there, the *Harlan Daily Enterprise,* give a pretty good account of the trouble.

"Strikers Exchange Gunshots with Private Guards and Local Law Enforcement" was the headline, and it went on to tell how the new sheriff come down on the side of the mining company and hauled eight miners off to jail for murder and attempted murder. The paper called it "the battle of Murder Creek," reminding me of the place Devil Jim was found hanging from a sycamore tree. Anyhow, the way the sheriff told it was he'd sent three cars, each one holding one of his deputies and a Baldwin-Felts man, to escort a busload of them scabs out to the Evarts mine.

They got waylaid and Elihu Simpson, one of the sheriff's new deputies, returned fire. But he was shot and killed on the spot, and after that, all hell broke loose. The striking miners, deputies, and gun thugs went at it, firing a thousand rounds at one another, the paper said, 'til all three of the deputies and one miner laid dead. (The Baldwin-Felts men must've been better at ducking and hiding, 'cause it never mentioned none of them being hit.)

The new sheriff made it sound like the miners was nothing but a bunch of hell-bent killers and was quoted saying things like, "My men never had a chance," and "They was ambushed by a dozen or more assailants who fired the first shots from in hiding near the depot."

Now, I weren't there, but that sounds like some pretty high talk for a county sheriff, and I have my suspicions somebody else might've put them words in his mouth— maybe one of them association fellers. I don't know.

But one part of the story did make me smile. It was right at the end where the sheriff was talking about what they'd done with the miners they arrested.

"According to Sheriff Blair," it said, the men was "remanded over to Lester Ball, the county jailer," and it done my heart good to read that and find out Lester had somehow managed to survive the politics and keep his job. I don't know, but I figure it might've had something to do with the judge there in Harlan—the one Boyd was friendly with—or maybe Lester just knowed too much to be fired, like maybe where all the bodies was buried.

Jack Grimes was right about one thing, though, they was a war that come to Harlan County that year and plenty of men died. It went on right up until the coal business started to peter out on account of what the newspapers called the Great Depression. What happened was, the

coal companies went bust—or most of them anyway—
and the miners got laid off, which pretty much put a end
to the union and the 'sociation both at the same time. By
my reckoning, we was lucky the union never made it into
Bell County. If they had, we might've ended up with our
own "Murder Creek."

Coal stayed big in the county for a time but never
come back like it was before the Depression. Moonshine
held steady, though, as you might expect—in spite of me
busting up every still I could find over all them years.

Anyhow, the years rolled by and next thing I knowed,
like Job in the Bible, I felt "old and full of days" and
ready to retire after twenty-five year as Bell County sheriff. That's twenty-five years of serving warrants, collect-
ing back taxes, and dealing with county politics, all the
while parking every morning in that same gravel lot behind the courthouse in front of that same faded old
"SHERIFF" sign that somebody nailed to the light pole
long before I.D. was sheriff and maybe even Guy Jackson
before him.

Pineville stayed pretty much the same as it was, but
I.D., Virgil, Judge Newsom, and every one of them old
fellers I owed my career to was all long dead by the time I
put my badge in the desk drawer for the last time. Even
Floyd had retired as chief of police by then.

That ain't to say I was done for, though. That following year, after I retired as sheriff, I run for mayor and won
the job hands down.

But that's another story for another day . . .

ACKNOWLEDGMENTS

Many thanks to the friends and family who encouraged me during the writing of this and the two preceding books in the FIREDAMP trilogy.

A debt of gratitude is due Dave ("*me*-Dave") Malone for his consistent encouragement and editorial advice, which included a well-placed "kick in the pants" at the appropriate moment.

Special thanks go to Thomas M. Hardwick for taking an interest in my research for the books and revealing to me the *true* identity and fascinating career of FBI Special Agent L.C. Schilder.

ABOUT THE AUTHOR

J. Kyle Johnson exchanged his technical hat for a creative one following a career of more than thirty years with science and engineering contractors of the federal government. He now lives in retirement among the beautiful mountains and lakes of East Tennessee with his lovely wife of nearly fifty years, the "Little Suzi" of the stories found at *jkylejohnson.net*. Born in Pineville, Kentucky, but raised in Oak Ridge, Tennessee, he earned his bachelor's and master's degrees at Tennessee Tech University.

THE FIREDAMP SERIES

by J. KYLE JOHNSON

Inspired by actual characters and events of 1930 Appalachia, the FIREDAMP series, set in the coal-mining region of Eastern Kentucky, follows the early career of Sam Garrett, an earnest young deputy thrust into the role of acting sheriff of Bell County following the shooting that seriously wounds the county sheriff. Added to the deputy's woes are run-ins with his wayward brother "Tick," who embroils him in his far-reaching acts of lawlessness; Dewey Grimes, a cruel and dangerous local bootlegger and his elusive son "Jack"; Lovis Evans, a contentious county coroner; and, eventually, coal mine operators in Harlan County, the infamous site of a bloody "war" that erupts between miners and local officers of the law there.

FIREDAMP
A Killing at Kettle Island
***

Firedamp is the fast-moving, first-person tale of a young deputy sheriff's struggle with ruthless bootleggers and crime bosses. Adding to his troubles are his ne'er-do-well brother, Billy Wade, known locally as "Tick," and his brother's "woman," Jonetta, an exotic Melungeon vamp. The story begins with the shooting of the county sheriff, then spins off into the investigation of a brutal killing at a coal mine in Kettle Island, where a firedamp (or flash fire) in a deep mine is somehow connected to the murder of a newly arrived miner.

HUNTER'S MOON
The Drownings at Pickerin Hollow
***

Hunter's Moon follows Sam Garrett's debut in *Firedamp* as a young deputy sheriff taking over for his mentor, I.D. Atkins, who has been sidelined by a bootlegger's bullet in Bell County, Kentucky. In this sequel, Sam returns to Pineville after doing battle with gangsters in Cincinnati and Newport, Kentucky—the original "Sin City" of its time—only to become entangled with a local moonshiner out for revenge after the deputy removes the man's abused children from a run-down shack in Pickerin Hollow.

MURDER CREEK
A Hanging at Bloody Harlan
***

Murder Creek, the third and final book of the *Firedamp* series finds Deputy Sheriff Sam Garrett once again in search of his prodigal brother "Tick" (Billy Wade) while at the same time wrestling with his conscience over allowing Jack Grimes (*Hunter's Moon*) to escape responsibility for the shooting death of his own father, the outlaw moonshiner Dewey Grimes. Sam revisits his cousin *me*-Curt, who advises him to drop the case against Jack, and recrosses the swinging bridge to Stoney Fork, where he receives an enigmatic warning from Mammy in the form of one of her "visions." In the meantime, Sam receives yet another unexpected call from Special Agent L.C. Schilder of the federal Bureau of Investigation in Cincinnati that sends him into the unfamiliar and dangerous territory of Harlan County, where the escalating conflict between the mining companies "association" and the miners union threatens to catch the deputy in the cross-hairs of hostilities.

Made in the USA
Columbia, SC
29 June 2021